Blood & Water

Katie O'Rourke

Brown House Books

Brown House Publishing
www.katieorourke.com

Copyright © Katie O'Rourke 2017

This is a work of fiction. Names, characters, places and events either are products of the author's imagination or are used fictitiously, and any resemblance to actual person's living or dead, business establishments or locales is purely coincidental.

Also by Katie O'Rourke

Monsoon Season
A Long Thaw
Still Life and other stories
Finding Charlie

For Kim and Debbie – my people.

"I know there's strength in the differences between us
And I know there's comfort where we overlap."
-Ani Difranco

Delilah: Tuesday, October 17th 2017

It isn't yet dawn as I ransack my apartment for things I can't leave behind. The list is surprisingly short.

Handfuls of clothing stuffed into a duffel bag. My laptop. An awkwardly-sized cardboard box full of nostalgia, the only things I'd allowed myself to take from my parents' house after my mother died. I wrap both arms around it, hefting it onto my hip as I cast my eyes in nervous darting circles, contemplating what doesn't make the cut. The futon. The microwave. Sheets and towels and curtains. I leave it all.

Everything fits quite easily in my Mini Cooper, the box and the duffel bag smooshed together on the backseat like sleepy children apprehensive of the spontaneous road trip. I go back to lock up, remembering to take a pale blue scarf from the hook just inside the door. I drape it over my fleece, which I zip up to my chin on the way back to the car. I slide into the front seat and turn the key. It starts right up – nothing like nightmares and old movies, where people can never leave in a hurry when they need to. Everything goes smoothly. Leaving is easy. As I pull out of the lot, and my apartment building gets smaller in the rearview, my breathing slows. I'm certain I won't miss any of it. I wonder why I never thought of this before.

I feel no attachment to material things. I take some degree of pride in that. Near the end of her life, my mother asked me to take her antique furniture. She had an oak dresser and nightstand that were a set and she didn't want them separated. She was dying and she was worried about keeping the furniture together.

After the funeral, there'd been an estate sale. I don't believe in an afterlife so I don't believe my mother is upset with me or proud of me or looking out for me.

Dead is dead.

The cardboard box contains twelve file folders that hold report cards and artwork and essays from every year I went to school. If I looked closely, I'm sure I'd find my SAT scores. I haven't looked closely, though. I saved a shoebox full of loose photos, but I haven't looked closely at those either. When I first lifted the lid in the basement, my throat started closing. I replaced the lid and set it aside. For later. Whenever that is.

My mother died five years ago, six months after being diagnosed with lung cancer. She'd never smoked. My father had smoked, though he quit before I was born. He'd died before her diagnosis. A heart attack we hadn't seen coming. She'd just begun to shake off the most crippling parts of her widowhood when she got the news that she wouldn't need to get used to living without him after all.

My father's death was sudden and shocking and devoid of the opportunity to say goodbye. It was terrifyingly fast: the fear in his eyes, his twisted face, the ambulance sirens too late. My mother's death was miserably slow, an endless terror with a million goodbyes until there was nothing left to say and nothing left to do but wait for the guilty relief when it was over.

Tucked into a corner of that box, wrapped in a checkered kitchen towel, are their wedding rings and her quarter carat diamond in yellow gold, the only jewelry my mother owned.

As I wait at the intersection on the way to the highway, remembering my favorite frying pan with grooves in it that made burgers look like they'd been grilled, I see a police cruiser in my rearview mirror. It turns into the parking lot of my apartment complex and I take a right on red.

You're having a panic attack.

This is what I say to myself in an attempt to be reassuring. It doesn't actually seem like that should be a comforting thought, but it is, because at least I'm not dying. It certainly feels like my heart is about to burst and I'm sure the oxygen has been sucked from the room, leaving me wheezing. But it's just a panic attack. It's horrible and terrifying, but, hey, it could be worse. I'll be fine. Eventually.

There's a knock on the door and my heart rate goes up even more. I'm sitting on a toilet in the family/disabled bathroom at Target with neither a family nor a disability. I'm holding my clammy head in my hands, talking to myself about breathing and other supposedly involuntary mechanics of the human body.

Count to ten. They'll just have to wait.

Another knock.

"Just a minute?" My voice is squeaky and high. I'm dizzy from the sacrifice of breath that comes from speaking.

Rushing just makes it worse. Breathe.

I reach for the toilet paper but my hands are numb so I paw at the roll until it spins.

I flush, go to the sink, run the water, look up.

It's not so bad.

I take a baseball cap out of my bag. It's not mine; I look stupid in hats. But the visor shades the deepening purple around my eye and when I suck in my lower lip, you can't even see that it's split.

I turn off the faucet and look myself in the eyes. It's all there: the disgust and self-pity and blame. My heartbeat has slowed.

Get out of here. Now.

The young mother on the other side of the door is so relieved when I exit, she hardly gives me the stink eye I deserve as she pulls her desperate five-year-old inside and I slip past, keeping my head down.

I leave Target empty-handed. I was going to get supplies for the trip, but I'd left my cart in the make-up aisle after catching a glimpse of myself in a mirror. The bruises were darkening fast and I was sweating. Trying to keep from having a panic attack in public feels like that movie, Teen Wolf, like you don't want everyone to find out you're really an animal.

Once when we were making up after a fight, Marty told me he felt like an animal sometimes. I tamed him. We'd been together for three tumultuous years. Loving him felt like a calling. He needed me. He said once that he knew I was good for him, but he wasn't sure he was good for me. I held him tighter and told him not to be so silly.

I should have listened to him then.

My car is parked close; the store wasn't open when I arrived. The plan was to load up on juice and power bars so I wouldn't be tempted by fast food chains.

I sit behind the wheel and take several deep breaths. I make a new plan.

I'll stop for snacks once I've passed a state line or two, once I've put some distance between me and the damage that's been done.

There are consequences to sticking around.

The first night, I find a dirt road in the woods and I sleep in my car. It's too cold to crack the windows after dark, but with them up, I feel like I might suffocate. I crawl into the backseat and try to sleep curled up on my side since there isn't room to stretch out. The middle of nowhere is noisier than you think it will be and the night is such a disaster, I vow to splurge on a motel room the next night.

On the road, I listen to my music. Not his. Marty was a music theory major and had very pretentious ideas about music. I am of the opinion that musical taste is entirely subjective, like with literature or food. If you like lima beans, it isn't because you're stupid or wrong – you just have different taste buds.

Marty thought my music was bad – like, in an absolute, definitive way. And his music was good. So, I got used to Bishop Allen and the Avett Brothers and The Smiths. Turns out, all the good music is by men.

I find a motel in Missouri for forty-five dollars. I pay cash and curse my cheapness the moment I let myself into the room. I'm afraid to sleep in the bed, convinced that it's infested with bed bugs, so I dress in long pants with my socks pulled over the cuffs and a hoodie with the strings cinched under my chin.

The parking lot is full and the walls are thin. The security lock on my door feels as secure as a paperclip holding together two sheets of notebook paper. I felt safer in my car.

I lie in bed unable to sleep until I'm so tired I don't care if someone breaks in to murder me.

When I wake, the parking lot is nearly empty. It doesn't make me feel safer; now there are just fewer people to hear me scream. Still, I force myself to take a shower, quickly, and take a complimentary cup of coffee from the lobby before I go.

Marty was thirty-seven when we met; he just turned forty last month. We celebrated with three of his buddies at the bar where they'd played gigs when they were in their twenties. The owner let them do a set in between two other acts. The audience was small and bored, but they cheered politely and no one was drunk or ornery enough to boo.

Not that they were horrible, just rusty. Marty's band consisted of aging musicians who once thought they might get famous doing this. Now they were still scrambling to find other ways to make a living, most of them drinking too much. On our first date, Marty had described his relationship with alcohol in a way that sounded like an active alcoholic. His theory was that the cold-turkey approach wasn't really necessary. He knew he was unable to stop after two beers, so his solution was that he didn't keep alcohol in the house. That way, he only drank on weekends.

As I listened to his story, I thought to myself that this was a red flag. In fact, I reasoned, this meant I could not date him. The disappointment of that realization struck me. We'd been having such a good time. He was easy to talk to, told good stories, made me laugh.

And I thought: What do I know about alcoholism? Nothing. Maybe he was right.

He wasn't. But by the time I'd figured that out, I was already in love with him.

I sleep in my car again on the third night, in a parking lot near Albuquerque, expecting to be woken by a police officer or a mugger pounding on the window. Instead, it's just the sunrise warming my face, hinting at the afternoon temperatures it's capable of.

This morning, I have to face facts. I spread the map across the counter at a Waffle House and give up the pretense that I've just been headed aimlessly "out west". Everything is west of the coastal town I started from, that smidgeon of New Hampshire that touches the Atlantic. It isn't until Albuquerque that I admit to myself that I have a destination. I'll need to take the dip south on I-10 to get there.

I don't call first. What would I say?

I have his address from the last Christmas card and the GPS system I borrowed from Marty a week ago. Mine now.

I'm so in my head I don't notice exactly when the landscape changes. The mountains in the distance hadn't been visible in the dark the night before. The saguaros are a kind of cactus I've read about. It takes fifty years for them to grow an appendage, though I'm suddenly skeptical of my data. There are many scattered along the foothills with five or seven "limbs" jutting in awkward angles from the main trunk. I prefer the ones with only two. They stand along the side of the road like men with their arms up, as if they're being held at gunpoint or perhaps warning me to slow down, beware.

The sun is setting as I park in front of his house. It's white stucco and there are low bushes with yellow flowers along the walk. I have no idea what any of the plants here are called, besides the cactus. But I don't see any of those in the manicured front yard. No grass either though, just pink pebbles.

I check out my shiner in the rearview. It's faded, but I reach for the baseball cap anyway. Just in case.

The garage door is closed and no one answers the bell. I sit on the front step and smooth my skirt over my knees. If I was in New England, I'd be reaching for a sweater now, but this is Tucson. After a day trapped in the car with recycled air, it feels nice to sit out in the breeze.

I imagine how it will be when he drives up and sees me here. Will he recognize me? It's been years and I'll be out of context, having never ventured this far from my home. It'll be confusing and dramatic, but he'll surely be happy to see me. We may not be what other people call close, but I've always felt we had a special connection. "Delilah!" he'll say. "What a surprise!"

He's the only person who calls me Delilah. It's my name, true, but even my parents called me Lilah. Kids at school mostly called me Dee, especially out on the soccer field. More efficient for shouting directions. Marty always called me Li, pronounced like the telling of a falsehood or like what you do on a bed before fucking.

So, pretty much the same thing.

When David calls me "Delilah", it makes my stomach clench, the way it did when I was little and in trouble. It was "Delilah Jane" on those occasions. He'd know that if he spent any amount of time in New Hampshire while I was growing up. He hadn't. By the time I was born, he'd already moved away.

The last time I'd seen him was five years ago, at our mother's funeral.

Nothing ever happens the way I imagine it. I spend forty-five minutes sitting on that step, slouching against the front door with my legs splayed out in front of me when a truck pulls up in front of the house and a teenage girl climbs out. The driver waits as she approaches me slowly.

I jump up and she steps back.

"Sadie!"

She scowls at the sound of her name.

"It's Lilah," I say, pressing my palm to my chest. "Delilah. Your aunt?"

She's still pouting, uncertainly. She wears every thought bare on her face.

"I haven't seen you since you were a tiny thing." She was a baby and wouldn't remember. David came home that Thanksgiving with his pretty wife and new daughter. That was so long ago, before the divorce. I'd seen photos since then but even those were outdated: pigtails and missing teeth. Here she is grown taller, long dark hair falling around her shoulders and dark eyes narrowed at me.

"I'm your dad's little sister," I say and she sighs, turns to the truck and waves them off.

"I think I've seen a picture of you," she says and she walks past me to unlock the door.

David: Friday

I'm a coward.

I'm taking the long way home from work even though it was after six before I finally left. I tell myself I can use the drive to think over the right thing to say, even though I've had all week to think of what to say. I've put it off until Friday so she'll have time to process it: to get upset, slam doors, regroup.

I'm managing the crisis.

At a red light, I lean my head back and close my eyes. I'm clenching my jaw with the same level of force that presses the brake pedal.

A week ago, Sadie came home all excited about her college applications. Her guidance counselor had told her she was selling herself short with the list of colleges she'd decided to apply to. With her grades, she could consider more than just state schools. Her new list had universities on the east coast or the mid-west, private colleges with impressive reputations exceeded only by their astronomical tuitions.

I nodded at her enthusiasm, a knot in my stomach. I wanted to remind her how excited she'd been about the University of Arizona, which was right in town. I knew, though, that too much talking it up might send her in another direction.

Sadie's guidance counselor had sent her home with a worksheet to fill out with her parents. It didn't need to be returned, it claimed, it was intended to start the discussion. There were two blank lines for contributions: one for me, one for her mother.

I tried calling her counselor from the privacy of my bathroom, but it went to voicemail. Through gritted teeth, and at a low volume, I had a rambling argument with a machine. "You don't know the situation!" I said three times before deleting the message and getting on with the weekend.

The damage was done.

The car behind me beeps and my head snaps to attention. *Green means go, moron.* Even my inner voice takes sides with the other driver. I ease onto the highway and the car shoots past me, emphasizing their annoyance.

Ahead of me, the dark outline of the Santa Catalinas dissolves into the night sky. In just a few hours, the mountains will disappear completely, their daytime beauty rendered irrelevant by the unstoppable turning of the earth.

All week, I'd been running the numbers. Maybe I could sell the house. I didn't need all this space especially once Sadie left. That worksheet was a joke, and not a nice one. I knew only one of those lines would ever be filled in.

Janet and I divorced when Sadie was eleven and Janet moved back in with her mother in Reno. We had shared custody, but Sadie stayed with me. She spent a couple months of the summer out in Nevada. I was up to date on my alimony payments, but Janet had never paid child support. If she was a man, she'd be called a deadbeat.

The thing is, Sadie knows none of this. She's a child; it isn't for her to worry about.

That stupid guidance counselor mucked it all up. Before her brilliant bit of meddling, we'd had a plan. The University of Arizona is a good school. Sadie wanted to live on campus and I understood that was part of the experience. I'd lived in the dorms when I was her age; it was time. Sadie was growing up.

Next year. *Next* year; not now. It seems like Sadie is always being forced to grow up faster than she should and there's so little I can do about it. Less and less.

When I come into the house, I hear giggling. Sadie hadn't mentioned bringing a friend home and this changes my concept of how the evening will go. There's a loosening of my muscles that I don't want to acknowledge as relief.

They're in the kitchen. They look up from the table as I enter, say my hellos.

"Have you eaten?" I ask.

Sadie laughs. "Dad, you haven't even seen who's here."

I turn then to look more closely at the other girl and for a moment I feel disconnected from the earth. There, sitting next to Sadie, is my mother.

This is impossible for many reasons, not least of which is that my mother is dead. Also, this ghost of my mother is young, about the age she'd been when I was a boy. She's wearing a Red Sox cap like the one I'd worn nearly every day of my childhood.

I don't believe in ghosts, but this disconnect lasts just long enough to make me worry that I might be having a break down or a brain aneurysm.

As she stands, I blink and realize that, of course, it's not my mother. It's my sister, which is unusual for a different set of reasons.

"Delilah," I say stupidly as she hugs me. "What are you doing here?"

"I needed an adventure," she says. "So, I got in the car and started driving."

"Isn't that cool?" Sadie says.

As Delilah pulls away, her head tilts upward and I see it; the yellow-green smudge on her cheekbone that makes her look even more like our mother. She straightens her baseball cap, her dark curls jutting out messily.

I hope Sadie hasn't seen it.

We order a pizza because all the dinner options in the refrigerator are meant to feed two people. Sadie eats with us and fills any awkward silence, but once she's finished she goes off to her room.

Delilah leans back in her chair. "I can't believe she's off to college next year."

I collect the empty plates, carry them to the sink. "Time flies." It's one of those clichés that couldn't be truer. It only ever startles people who don't have children.

"No kidding." Delilah gathers the crumpled napkins and puts them in the trash.

She turns. I'm leaning against the counter. We've run out of small talk.

"Is someone looking for you?" I ask.

She tips her head uncertainly and I touch my face where hers is bruised.

She sighs. "I don't think so." She sounds disappointed.

"I need to know if there's a danger of some jerk showing up here. I have Sadie to consider."

"It's not what you're thinking."

I nod. I've heard that before. I imagine she'll be back with him by next week.

Delilah yawns and I look at my watch. "You must be tired. I'll make up the guest bed."

"I can do it. Just give me the sheets." We argue clumsily and I persuade her to let me do it while she showers. I head to the back of the house and she goes out to her car to bring in some of her things. I want to ask how long she plans to stay, but I can't figure out a way to say it that won't sound like I want her to leave.

After her shower, she comes to say goodnight wearing sweats and smelling of Sadie's raspberry shower gel. With her damp hair slicked back, she looks less like a grown up and more like my kid sister.

We didn't grow up together so I've always experienced her aging at an accelerated rate. She had an extremely rapid babyhood while I was in college. I'd return in the summers and she'd be a whole new little person. She was twelve in my wedding pictures, her mouth full of metal, seventeen the year I took Janet and Sadie home for Thanksgiving. The next time I went back was after the divorce and by then, Delilah had moved out on her own.

The last time I saw her, her hair had been tied back and pinned down as if her curls were too whimsical for the occasion. For the first time, she looked old; she wore a shapeless black dress, the skin of her face drooped and sagged. I'd never seen her wear make up; my mother used to complain about it.

"A little lipstick goes a long way," she'd say. Delilah just laughed at her, never seemed to let it hurt her feelings. If Janet ever said something like that to Sadie, I'd be irate.

"Thanks for letting me stay," Delilah says now.

"Of course." I get up from the couch and as I hug her, she tucks her head under my chin and I'm struck by her smallness. "Stay as long as you need."

When I go to bed, there's still light coming from under Sadie's closed door. Last year, I was still enforcing a lights out by eleven policy, but I stopped doing that over the summer. She needs to learn how to manage her time, set her own sleep schedule. You give your kids all the tools and then you have to step back and hope they learned how to use them.

She only spent three weeks in Nevada this summer, in July. Janet said she couldn't afford to keep her all summer, couldn't afford airfare either. So, I drove her down July 4th weekend, feigning plans with an old college buddy in Vegas. And I let her think she'd won an argument, wanting to spend most of her summer in Tucson with her friends. She begged me to break it to her mother and when I said I would, she said "thank you, Daddy!" even though she hadn't called me that since she was ten.

I love my daughter, but it hurt to lose my summer, the only part of the year when I'm free to behave like other single men my age. Not just a single parent, but a single person. Some summers I join Match.com. That first year, I took a motorcycle training class, as if I'd ever buy a motorcycle. It was a fun weekend fantasy and only cost $300. I was a better rider than I thought I'd be. I passed the exam. But all that really came of it was a friendship I'd formed with the instructor, Tim. I'd run into him a week later at Vintage Bike Night, a bi-monthly event at a local brew pub.

Tim told stories with a glass of Red Cat Amber in hand. He only ever drank one, needing to stay alert for the ride home, ever the responsible role model for the newbies who met up on Wednesdays. The crowd was different on those nights: students from class mingling with members of Tucson's motorcycling community. I made it a point to go all summer, even though the class was over and I'd let go of the pretense of becoming one of them. Tim had ridden his motorcycle around the world in 2011. He had been in Egypt at the start of the Arab Spring. He'd busted a tire in Kazakhstan. He'd been invited to spend a night with a family in Mongolia.

We've been friends for close to six years. It's funny to think about what stuck and what didn't. I'm still driving an SUV with dual airbags and haven't managed to string more than three dates together with the same woman since Janet. But I made a friend. Not a small thing.

There's only one summer left and then Sadie will be off. Somewhere. And I'll be free to fill my time in interesting ways again.

But for now, it's past eleven on a Friday night and I'm dead tired.

In the morning, Sadie sleeps in as usual. Delilah is already up, huddled over a cup of coffee at the kitchen table. "I'm still on East Coast time," she says, in lieu of a greeting.

I wrestle with the Keurig and she doesn't force conversation until I'm caffeinated. When I was a child, my mother was always the first one up. She'd make the coffee and get me settled in front of the TV, watching cartoons at a low volume. She cooked my father eggs every day, bacon on weekends. She made his breakfast even on the days he wasn't working, which was frequent and sporadic. She cooked for him on the mornings he was hungover, the mornings she moved carefully, favoring her left hand, holding her ribs, wincing when she reached for the juice glasses.

I sit across from Delilah and ask how she slept, what her plans are for the day.

"I was thinking I might take a walk," she says. "I'm surprised it's so cool this morning."

"That's October. It'll warm up, though, so you probably want to go sooner rather than later." It occurs to me that I can talk to Sadie while she's out. "We're right near the river walk."

"That sounds nice."

There's a lull. I struggle to remember what she does for work. Something non-profit-y. Since our mother died, I no longer get detailed updates. I heard something from her at Christmas. She sent Sadie a book she'd loved when she was in high school, something by a woman I'd never heard of.

"How's the job?" I ask, vaguely, hoping it isn't obvious that I've forgotten what it is.

She sinks a bit in her seat and sighs, caving in and deflating before my eyes. "I'm sort of between things," she says. "It's a bad time to be in social services. States are making cut backs, grants we're used to getting are suddenly denied, and the programs are gone. Nothing to do."

I groan and shake my head. "It's terrible the way the most vulnerable are the first to pay when the wealthy fuck everything up."

She shrugs. "Yep."

"So, what's next for you?" I ask.

She gazes past me out the glass doors to the patio. "I'm not sure yet."

When I was seventeen, I was an only child. I picked a college with a good engineering program and a low tuition, on the other side of the country. We had a plan, my mother and I, and though it had never been spoken out loud, I was confident. I did my part.

Once I was on my own, my mother would be free. With grants and academic scholarships, I was able to take care of myself. She didn't have to worry. When I flew home that first Thanksgiving, my mother picked me up in the green station wagon and took me to lunch and I prepared myself for her to break the inevitable news: she was leaving him.

I imagined that eventually, she'd move to California to be closer to me, get a little apartment with a fenced-in patio, learn to garden.

We unwrapped our subs across from each other as she told me she had a little surprise.

I remember thinking that was a weird way to say it. I wasn't going to be upset, sure, but I'd expected she'd find a more respectful tone. We'd put on a show for each other: it was a difficult but necessary thing.

I was still expecting to hear the word divorce when, instead, she beamed at me and said: "We're having a baby."

As I sputtered and forced her to repeat herself, she reached for my hand across the table. Her other hand rested on her stomach.

As she chattered on, I felt myself turning gray. She was wearing a cream, cable knit sweater, too bulky for me to judge how far along she might be. I had a surge of hopefulness as a thought occurred to me and I blurted it out: "You don't need to go through with it."

She snatched her hand away and narrowed her eyes. "We're having a baby," she said again, slowly, pronouncing each word separately.

"But now you'll never get away from him."

"I was never getting away, dear. He's my husband."

"But his drinking—"

She held up her hand to shush me. "He's not drinking anymore. He's given it up."

"For now."

"It's different this time," she said and she rubbed her stomach again.

The idea that he'd stop drinking for this child filled me with contempt. First, for my mother for falling for it and then, as the years passed and my father stayed sober, for the child. She had managed what I never could.

Whenever I returned home, I was wary of this new man my

father had become. He changed diapers and read stories and sat on the floor of the playroom to *play*. Dolls and dress-ups and tea parties. He was a nice man, but no one I recognized. This was the same drunken bastard who had slammed me into the wall and punched through the sheetrock by my head when I had started getting big enough to step between him and my mother. Once he was sober, we began eyeing each other with a mutual unease. I remembered who he really was and I couldn't give in to the delusion that sobriety changed his essential character.

Delilah had never known that man.

I got married and found less and less time to visit. It was a relief that I didn't have to worry about my mother anymore and I was happy for her, but this new family was so unfamiliar to me. I never really felt a part of it.

When Delilah leaves, I ignore the knot in my stomach and knock on Sadie's door. She lowers the volume of her music before granting me entrance.

She's sitting at her desk, looking up at me expectantly. We picked out that desk together at Ikea. It took an entire Saturday, driving to Phoenix and wandering through the enormous blue warehouse. We had lunch at the cafeteria there. When I sit on the edge of her bed, her eyebrows furrow.

"There's something I have to talk to you about," I say and she crosses her arms. I can feel her steeling herself against whatever's coming.

Delilah: Saturday

It's a short walk to the edge of David's neighborhood and across one major street before I find the paved walking path along the river, though the river is barren. I hadn't realized that when he talked about it, but of course there's no water here. Back home, the earth is filled with the sound of water rushing or trickling through the green, even now when the leaves are dying their vibrant deaths. The water wouldn't be quiet until it froze.

I'm wearing the purple leggings and tank top I purchased for the kick boxing class my friend Leslie talked me into. She had a guest pass and I had a brief image of myself as someone who did those sort of things. Within twenty minutes, that image dissolved.

I should call her, but what would I say?

She never liked Marty. She was smart enough not to say so, but I could tell. We'd known each other for a decade, met when we'd both worked for Easter Seals. She'd gone back to school for her Masters in social work and was surviving the cuts. I'd never done that and I ended up working at a grocery store.

Until I lost that job too.

I can't call Leslie until I figure out how to spin it. She knows me too well, will hear it in my voice. It's more than the stupid job. I'll have to email her.

David tried to convince me to take a bottle of water and I didn't want to argue so I nodded and put it back in the fridge when he wasn't looking. I like to have my hands free. I make fun of people back home who carry water everywhere, but as my steps slow, I realize the desert really is different.

I'd like to sit and catch my breath, but I imagine rattlesnakes in the sand beyond the pavement. Instead, I stop and stretch my arms over my head, bending to the right and left, smiling as a cyclist comes whirring toward me and passes me without so much as a nod. It's like I'm not even there.

And I wonder: Do you still call something a river when it lacks the very thing that made it a river in the first place?

Last week, my boss came to speak to me after my lunch break. Business was slow; she had fewer and fewer hours to give me. When people started tightening budgets, organic vegetables and cage-free eggs were some of the first things to go. By the end of our conversation, I was the one trying to keep her together.

I went to Marty's house, knowing it was his day off. I drove there thinking about Leslie's advice these past months, going back to school. But, did it really make sense to double down on a career in social services in the current political climate?

The other obvious concern was how to go to school and keep paying my bills. Whenever we'd discussed moving in together, Marty would sigh as if the idea was too boring to put into words. "Aren't things great as they are?" he'd say.

And I had to admit I liked my privacy. Some mornings I didn't brush my teeth until after lunch. But was that worth paying rent at two places?

I could tell Marty wasn't home when I pulled into the driveway and his car was gone. I undid my seat belt and texted him: Where are you?

We didn't have each other's keys, but I knew where he kept the spare. I couldn't imagine he'd mind; it was not a typical day. And besides, I had to pee.

I let myself in, figuring I'd just use the bathroom and wait for him to text me back. If he was somewhere in town, I could go meet him. While I waited, I looked in his fridge, absent-mindedly opening the lid to a box of leftover pizza even though I wasn't hungry. It was pepperoni, which was weird.

Marty was a vegetarian.

I closed the door to the refrigerator. There were an infinite number of simple explanations for this, of course. That's what I told myself as I walked down the hallway to his bedroom. There, I found his bed was neatly made. Again, weird. Marty never made his bed.

I pulled my phone out and looked at the screen. No replies.

I sat on the bed, feeling queasy. The day was unsettling, that's all. Getting fired always sucked, even if it wasn't your dream job. On the desk in the corner, Marty's laptop was open (weird), the screensaver dancing. I stood and drew a finger across the touchpad. The screen snapped to life and I was looking at the Facebook page of a stranger. A blond female stranger named Lyndsy Parker.

I sat down in front of the screen as it slowly dawned on me: I wasn't just looking at her profile; I was logged into her account. Her most recent status update said: "Off to Applecrest with my honey!"

Several hours passed and by the time the sun went down, I knew a lot about Lyndsy and her honey. He was a fairly new part of her life; he'd gotten seven mentions since July. Never by name, but occasionally an initial: "M". There were no photos of him and only one of her, a cell phone selfie with sunglasses. I had just begun to pore over her friends' accounts when my cell phone chirped with Marty's text: I'm beat and going to bed early. We still on for tomorrow night?

I looked at the smooth expanse of Marty's bed, wondering where he was going to bed early.

I found my car keys on the table by the door and started driving.

I'm three houses away when I see Sadie burst out her front door, charging toward the sidewalk. Her face is twisted and I stop, wondering if I should turn away, pretending not to have seen her. I don't want to intrude on what manages to seem like a private moment, even if this is a public street in the middle of the day.

Sadie's headed right for me, although her head is down and she appears oblivious to the existence of anyone or anything outside the three-foot radius she's in the center of. She looks up before she crashes into me and I grab her upper arms, looking into her scrunched up little face.

"Sadie! What's wrong?"

"He's such a liar!" she chokes out and my first thought is that I hadn't realized she had a boyfriend. But, of course she would – such a pretty girl. David could only shelter her so much.

I pull her in for a hug and she lets me, burying her face into my shoulder and letting out a wail that makes me look around for disapproving neighbors. "Let's go back to the house," I say.

"No way! I don't even want to look at him!"

"Who?"

"My father!" She says it like a cuss word and I begin to realize I've misunderstood.

"How about we go for coffee? Just us girls."

She looks at me warily and I regret having added that last part.

She's too old for cutesie pandering.

She sighs and rubs her face. "Fine." She spins around, walks to my car and leans against the passenger's side while I go inside for the keys and tell David I've got it. Whatever that means. At any rate, he looks relieved as if he believes I'm the kind of person you can trust in a crisis. I used to be that person; I really did.

If I had it to do over again, I'd have only gone after his car. That had been my intention when I took the metal baseball bat from under my bed and drove back to his house. I have always had contempt for wives and girlfriends who waste their time being angry at the other woman, subjects of trashy talk shows instigating cat-fights. She's not the one who broke a promise to you. She didn't hold your hand by your parents' gravestones, swearing you'd never be alone. She didn't curl around your naked body, whispering secrets into your ear as night became day.

And yet, when I pulled up in front of Marty's house, her car in his driveway was all I could see.

By then, I'd spent hours driving around town, looking for him at all his local haunts and then ending up back where I'd started. If his driveway had been empty, I might have gone back to my apartment, burned some old photos, had a good cry, called Leslie. But it wasn't empty, was it?

There was her light turquoise Honda Civic, seeming adorable and uncomplicated and accommodating. As I slipped out of the silver Mini Cooper I'd be making payments on for several more years, I had tunnel vision for those rectangular tail lights.

My breath made smoke in the darkness. I remember the weight of the bat, pulling the muscles in my shoulders. I remember the sound of the glass smashing and tinkling on the pavement, crunching under my feet as I circled the car and started on the headlights. A light switching on as I moved on to the side windows.

The windshield didn't shatter on the first hit. The glass splintered like the top of crème brule beneath a spoon. It gave way with the second swing and caved in with a satisfying crash as the front door of the house banged open.

I saw her without really looking up, standing in the doorway in shorty shorts and a tank top, barefoot. She had blond hair that was cut close to her head and stood up in the back. She was squinting and slack-jawed, her face pale and feature-less, the kind of girl who has to draw on her eyebrows every morning.

She came at me before I could turn toward her and was on top of me. I heard the clang of the bat as it fell and rolled away from me, down down down the driveway. She sat on my back and mashed one side of my face into the pavement while smacking the other with her fists. She was yelling but I couldn't make out the words. One of the punches landed against my ear and it stopped working. The only sound was conveyed through the ear that was pressed to the ground.

I had never been in a physical fight – not even as a child, having grown up without siblings my age to tussle with. I didn't try to hit her back, just curled into a ball and focused on covering my vital organs.

Just when I thought I might pass out, her weight was lifted from me. I crawled away and turned to see Marty holding her around the waist as her arms and legs scrabbled and fought against him. He pulled her back and when he set her down, he pointed to her feet. They were bleeding.

I waited there, sitting on my ass in a driveway glittering with broken glass. I just watched as they conferred and he helped her inside. When he turned and came at me, I flinched. The three years we'd been together, he yelled but never hit me. I understood, though, that I had pushed things into another realm – one in which impossible things that had never happened before were possible. I prepared myself for the slap; part of me craved it.

But he just grabbed my upper arms and yanked me to my feet. He spun me around and gave me a shove with the meaty heel of his hand right between my shoulder blades. Through no will of my own, I tottered down the drive, the rotation of my knees mechanical as though I were simply a wind-up toy within a Rube Goldberg, performing my bit in the string of chain reactions.

At the bottom of the driveway, my body stopped its forward motion. I turned.

Marty was holding his head in his hands and rocking back and forth. "Get the fuck out of here, Li! The police are coming!"

As I got into my car, other lights in the neighborhood were coming on. I was halfway down the street before I remembered I'd left the bat behind.

I get most of the story in the car ride. Sadie's done crying; now she just slouches against the door and talks to her reflection in the window. It reminds me of car rides with my mom during my own adolescence.

Apparently, my brother has kept things from her. About her mother and child support and this means she can't go out of state for college. I don't completely understand the connection, but I'm afraid to ask questions. When I gently suggest he was only trying to protect her, she throws up her arms and starts shouting that she isn't a baby. I don't say anything else until we're settled at a corner table, our Chai teas in hand.

With the air conditioning, it's so much cooler inside than out. I huddle over my steaming mug, wishing I'd had time to change. Even though just about everyone in the café is wearing shorts, I feel out of place in so much Lycra.

"I thought you wanted to go to the University of Arizona," I say.

"The U of A is like a safety school," she says, blowing across the top of her mug. "It's like ten minutes from my house."

I roll my eyes. "Come on. It's a really good school." I know this because I applied and was rejected, ages ago. And I was a good student. I hadn't really wanted to go. I applied on a whim because David lived out here. But it caught me off guard because I expected them to want me. I was relieved when my acceptance to UNH came the week later.

"But I want to go away to college," Sadie whines.

I shrug and lean back in my chair. "College is like a whole new world. You'll be surprised how far away it can feel. I went to college a half hour from where I grew up. I only saw my parents if I came home to do laundry."

She scowls across the table, unconvinced.

"And you might even like having your dad nearby, like, in case of emergency."

Sadie shakes her head. "My dad just does not want me to grow up. If I'm in town, he'll be showing up all the time."

"So, you make ground rules." After my first semester, I called home to arrange the trip back for winter break and my dad joked that it seemed like they'd just dropped me off. I'd assumed it was a joke, but it occurs to me now that he might have liked his empty nest. David might too. I wonder if this has ever occurred to Sadie.

I sip my tea. "Have you looked into NAU? Is that far enough away?" The college in Flagstaff is several hours north in a part of Arizona that gets snow. "Maybe your sophomore year, you do a semester abroad."

Sadie's dark hair falls forward, a long strand across her pouting face. In the silent stalemate, our drinks cool and I catch odd snippets of conversation at the tables around us, other people living out their own dramas. Sadie reminds me of another girl I'd known years ago, a girl named Krissy who slouched across a desk at me as we talked about her future. Instead of semesters, we'd talked trimesters. Krissy wasn't destined for college. Few of the kids I'd worked with over the years were.

I sigh. "You have a father who really cares about you. A lot of people don't have that." I'm running out of patience for what passes for hardship in Sadie's privileged life. How do parents have the energy to listen to complaints on this scale? I toss back the last of my tea and slam the mug on the table like we're in a bar. "Having that makes you pretty fucking lucky."

Sadie blinks and is silent.

I recognize that startled expression; she hasn't heard a word I've said up to this moment, but now she's listening. At work, this was always the goal, to get their attention so you could build trust. It wasn't the breakthrough; it just made the breakthrough possible. I wonder if anything I ever did for those kids added up to anything useful.

I lean back and try again. "What do you want to be when you grow up?"

She shrugs. "I don't know." She casts her eyes around the café and then looks right at me. "Did you know when you were my age?"

I see it then; she isn't Krissy – she's me. That's what's making me so irritable. When I was seventeen, I had everything and I didn't even know it. I laugh. "Nah. I'm still not really sure."

While my mother was dying, she told me a story she'd never told me before. She said she'd never told anyone. I pulled my chair closer to her bedside, not totally sure I wanted to know. But our roles had reversed so I was taking care of her now; if she needed to unburden herself in her last days, it was my job to listen.

Before I was born, she told me, my father had been a very

different man. He drank and he got angry and he hit her.

"Sometimes," she said, her voice breaking, "he hit David."

"What?" My mind reeled. I wondered how much this revelation was related to the morphine.

She ploughed ahead, ignoring my distress and doubt. "I was so relieved when David went away to school. I thought I could handle it on my own, but I couldn't bear to see David hurt anymore or see the way he looked at me. Judging me. It worked better as a secret. I could live with it as long as no one knew."

"Mom?" She wasn't looking at me and I smoothed the wisps of hair across her forehead, willing her back.

It worked. She met my eyes and smiled the most heartbreaking smile. "But then I found out I was pregnant."

I nodded, smiling along, trying to ignore the *but*. "With me."

"With you." She squeezed my hand. "And I was terrified. I didn't know what else to do."

"What else?"

"I told Dr. Harmon I couldn't go through it again. I swore I was going to get an abortion if he didn't help me."

I pulled my hand away. I'd never heard her talk about my conception as anything other than wonderful. A wonderful surprise. When I was a sophomore in college, I'd had an abortion. It had never occurred to me to talk to my mother about it. I took it for granted that she'd never wrestled with such an idea. She'd been younger than me when David was born and she was already married. My mother had always been quite clear on her position: babies were blessings, even when they were unplanned.

"But you didn't have an abortion," I said, laughing uncertainly.

"No," she said. "Dr. Harmon had your father come in for a physical and told him the blood work showed liver distress. He told him that if he didn't stop drinking, he'd die."

"And that worked?"

She nodded and closed her eyes. "And everything was different after that."

When my father died, David hadn't made it back for the funeral. He was going through the divorce and somehow that made it impossible. He'd come a week later to be with my mother and I found reasons not to meet them for dinner.

Suddenly, I saw his absence differently.

At my mother's funeral, David sat beside me in the church and wept openly for the entire service.

Back at the house, David's in the garage with another man. A motorcycle is parked on the curb.

Sadie darts into the house before I've even got the key out of the ignition. I walk slowly up the driveway.

"I guess I'm not forgiven," David says as I pass through the open garage door.

I shrug. "She seemed calmer at least."

"This is my kid sister, Delilah," he says to the other man. "This is Tim."

Tim and I each take a step towards each other and shake hands. Again, I'm wishing for a different outfit. I step away and fold my arms across my chest.

"Nice to meet you," Tim says. He's dressed in motorcycle gear: black pants with reflective stripes up the sides. He's got a goatee and muscular arms beneath the thin fabric of a long sleeve jersey.

"That must be your ride," I say, nodding in the direction of his bike.

He smiles and nods; he's distracted. He explains that he just stopped by on his lunch break to drop something off. He apologizes for having to rush away so soon. "I hope we can talk more next time."

The idea that he's thinking hopefully about a future conversation with me makes my face feel warm and I look away to keep him from noticing. I'm an idiot, flirting with a stranger less than a week after the greatest heartbreak of my life.

I say goodbye hurriedly and slip into the house, leaving David to see him off. Curled up on the guest bed, I think about that word: heartbroken. Is that what I am? It's certainly not just that.

Marty was the lead singer in his band and wrote most of the lyrics. His list of songs were all women's names, but I never felt jealous. He'd explained to me that he only wrote songs about women after it was over.

I wonder if he's writing about me now.

Tim: Sunday

I sit on the edge of the bed and Sara's eyelashes flutter. She reaches for me in the darkness.

"I dreamed that you already said goodbye," she says.

"Not yet."

"And we sang a French song."

"Zoo-be, zoo-be, zoo," I murmur, a bad interpretation of a French song from a television show we watch.

She giggles with her eyes closed, shaking her head.

"It's the only French song I know."

She smiles, drifting back to sleep. I bend down to kiss her mouth. "I love you."

Her eyes flash open. "In the dream, you kissed me three times." She closes her eyes again and puckers her lips.

I kiss her twice more.

"I love you," she says.

I stand and lift the cat onto the bed. "Look who I found."

"Kitty." Sara runs her hand along Lola's spine.

"Have a good day."

"You too."

I get to the range before sun up and realize I've forgotten the gate key. The key I have is for the Conex on the other side, the small shipping container that holds the training bikes. I climb the fence and hope my white privilege keeps me from getting shot.

I've ridden motorcycles for fifteen years and never had an accident. It makes me perfect for my weekend gig: teaching people how to ride. Today is the second and final riding day for this class. There are seven men and three women, from the age of eighteen to seventy-two. Some are seasoned riders who just need an endorsement for their license, but some are brand new. According to the paperwork, one of the students has never even ridden a bicycle before. I don't understand how that's possible.

Before they went home yesterday, I told the students to get a good night's sleep. In their dreams, the lessons they learned would sink in and they'd come back with a better grasp on everything. I read that somewhere and it's a comforting thought, whether or not it's true.

I walk each of the training bikes over to the staging area and have just begun setting up the cones when my assistant coach shows up. Eddie has the gate key and a cup of coffee. He lets himself in and walks slowly toward me.

"You got that," he says, nodding at the pavement in front of me. It's not exactly a question.

"Almost done," I say and he sits down in the aluminum chair I dragged out of the Conex.

In my head, I beg him not to complain about the early hour. It's either this or sweating it out under the midday sun in Tucson. I know what I prefer. Eddie slouches in the chair with his cap tipped over his eyes. He doesn't get off his ass until the first car pulls in the lot, but it doesn't bother me. I like the quiet.

Winter is a thing of the past. Nearly all my childhood memories are in winter: building snow forts with the neighbor kids, shoveling the drive only to have to start over when the plow went by, sweating in a snow suit that made it hard to lift my arms. I learned to drive on black ice, steering into the skid, ignoring the instinct to slam on the brakes. I lost my virginity on an ice fishing trip; it all started because she was cold. My mother died the December I was seventeen, but they couldn't put her in the ground until spring and I was gone by then.

That's North Dakota for you. Surely there were summers, but I hardly remember them. It was January after high school graduation when I moved to Tucson. It was my friend Billy's idea, but I jumped at it. Christmas had been pathetic. My father put a tree in the living room and hauled the decorations up from the basement, but that box sat in the corner unopened. Neither of us could be bothered. It was still sitting there the morning I left, and it seemed there were more pine needles on the floor than the tree.

For all I know, it's still there. In the twenty-some-odd years since, I've never been back. I call once or twice a year. Neither of us has much to say. We never did.

Billy didn't even last through that first summer in Tucson. The heat seemed downright apocalyptic at the start. It's an adjustment, to be sure. I might have run back myself, but I had a girlfriend by then and a job that covered rent on my own. Before a year was up, the girlfriend had moved in.

Carly. Carly was a few years older than me and she had an ex-husband who'd cheated on her. She was jealous and insecure and I understood. When she followed me home from work or went through my wallet while I showered or slapped me that time I came home late, I understood. I thought her insecurity was a tough time we'd get past, that once I'd proven myself she'd relax. I spent more years trying to prove myself than she'd been married to the jerk. Seven years.

Toward the end, everything was a battle, but I couldn't remember it ever being otherwise. Our dysfunction felt normal.

I actually brought the cat home on a romantic whim, but Carly was just mad I hadn't asked her first. Spent the night locked in the bedroom, refusing to speak to me. In the morning, to appease her, I let her name it. We finally broke up hardly a week later and I thought of changing it, but it didn't seem fair to the cat. She was already used to it. So was I.

I felt so free when Carly left, I got an ear pierced, stopped shaving, and bought a motorcycle.

David's already seated when I get to the restaurant and I slide into the booth across from him, setting my helmet on the seat beside me.

"How was class?" he asks.

I shrug. "No one crashed; no one died." I pick up the menu, one of those big, laminated corporate jobbies. Everything's corporate around here. The décor on the wall has been focus-grouped, designed to make you feel like you're having a unique dining experience. But it's exactly the same as the ones in Spokane, Nashville and Tallahassee. I'm not a fan of chains, but David's a picky eater so I let him choose the place. Seems all my friends are picky eaters these days. Zach with his diabetes and Julio suddenly "watching his weight." Maybe it's our age. I've started reading labels at the grocery store, checking the sodium. Never used to do that.

I order a bacon cheeseburger; David gets a salad. "Sadie got you on a diet?" I ask. He'd gone vegan for a while once, to support her. We were all glad when she gave that up.

"Nah. She's not even talking to me right now."

"What's she mad about?" I remember her pouting when I saw her the day before, but I hadn't had time to ask. I just figured it was generic adolescence. I've known Sadie since she was ten or eleven. She's a good kid, smart, but she knows how to manipulate her father. Has him wrapped around her little finger.

"The stuff about the child support came out. Because of college applications."

"That's rough." The waitress comes with our sodas. "But I guess it was just a matter of time, right?"

"I almost made it."

"One more year 'til you're free, man." I lift my glass in a toast and he lifts his, but I can tell his heart's not in it. "Can't protect her forever." The *her* is purposely nonspecific. Is it Sadie or Janet he's protecting? Hard to say. That woman left him with all the work of parenting after the divorce. I hadn't known him when they were still married, but from the sounds of it, she'd abdicated her responsibilities long before that. David had stepped up, though. He's a good dad.

As if on cue, he pulls his phone from his back pocket to scan for messages and then places it face up on the tabletop. In case she breaks her silence, I guess. He's always on call.

"Course it's me she's mad at – not her mother," he says. "When I said she could ask Janet about it, she said she didn't want to put that kind of pressure on her mom. She doesn't seem to worry about the pressure I'm under."

"Take it as a compliment: you're the parent she trusts. She doesn't have to take care of you."

He grunts and nods. "Delilah said something along those lines."

"How's that been?" I think of the woman I'd met the day before with wild hair and incongruous work-out attire. Her wardrobe didn't seem to match her personality. I'd only spoken to her briefly, but David had mentioned her arrival had been unexpected.

"It's been nice to see her, to have her get to know Sadie. I'm a bit worried about her."

"Worried?"

"I get the feeling she's running away from something. Or someone."

"Ah, well. Haven't we all been there?"

Before he can answer, the food comes. I think Tucson is filled with people running away from something, the way everyone you meet is from somewhere else. It occurs to me that David may never have run away from anything in his life. Maybe he's always been the kind to face things head-on.

"You and Sara should come to dinner this week," he says when the waitress has left.

"Cool." I reach for the ketchup. "It'll just be me, though. Sara's flying back east tomorrow."

"Doesn't she usually go in the summer?"

"Yeah. There's a wedding on Saturday so she pushed her annual pilgrimage. I hope it doesn't get too cold. She doesn't own a winter coat."

Sara moved to Tucson a decade ago and she'd tossed all her winter gear. She visited the east coast in the summer, pretty much exclusively, when it was sunny and humid. I went back with her two years ago and she'd delighted showing me around a place I'd never been before. We ate lobster rolls and lobster bisque and lobster pie. The last night of our trip, her friend Ally boiled lobsters in a pot and Sara taught me how to crack their shells and pull the sweetest meat from the tail.

"How's the internet dating?" I ask. David opened a Match.com account this summer and has yet to close it.

He shrugs. "Fine. I seem to manage to fit in a date every couple weeks."

"Any second dates?"

"Nope." He laughs bitterly. "I spend more time reading profiles than actually going out. And, you know what I can't understand? I'm looking at women in my age bracket and a lot of them say they've never been married, no kids. How does that happen?"

He says this to me: a man past forty, unmarried, no kids. "Hmm, yeah. I can't imagine." I think he'll hear the sarcasm in my voice, but he just keeps shaking his head. I stare at him and wait for it to dawn on him. It doesn't. I go back to my burger as he rambles on.

"And what would we talk about?"

I shrug. "You could ask her what interesting things she's been able to do since she hasn't been saddled with kids, what she spends all that extra money on." He looks up and it seems to occur on him finally. I've known this guy for six years and somehow we've managed to find things to talk about. "Seriously, all it means is that she didn't settle for the wrong guy. You want to hold that against her?"

He offers a glum smile. "Kinda."

Sara's on the couch when I get home, curled up with her laptop. Three days ago, she cut her dirty blond hair short and it's still catching me by surprise. I'm used to the messy pony tail; now it stops at her chin and falls across her forehead, too short to tuck behind her ears. That part's driving her crazy. "How was class?" she asks.

"No one crashed; no one died." I kiss her and sit down beside her while I pull off my boots.

"Did everyone pass?"

"Yep."

"Even the old guy?"

"He did really well."

She nods approval. Last night, I told her about how he'd confided that he was a widower and was trying to find ways to fill his time. His kids thought he was crazy. I knew Sara was rooting for him.

"New shirt?" I ask. Her wardrobe is generally jeans and a solid colored top. She goes for shades of blue and gray. Black. Sometimes, purple. She dresses like someone trying to blend in and not draw attention.

She looks down at herself. Her shirt is a deep red with pink polka-dots. "Yeah. You like it?"

"I do. I'd borrow it."

She grins and shakes her head. "You'd stretch it out with your manly arms."

I smile as I lean my head back, close my eyes. "You ready for your trip?"

"Let's not talk about it."

Sara hates flying.

"It'll be fine," I say and I squeeze her hand.

"I know." She squeezes back.

Sara: Monday

I sit in the front row by the window. The bulk-head seating. Since there's nowhere to put my carry-on baggage, the flight attendant insists that everything go in the overhead compartment, including my little purse, which is about the size of a submarine sandwich. Later, when the announcement is made that the flight is full and therefore: "All lap infants must be on laps," I'll wonder why they're not forced into overhead bins as well. In the event of "an emergency landing," I prefer to imagine my purse as a loose object rather than flying babies.

I'm grateful when the woman sitting next to me promptly falls asleep. On the first leg of the trip, from Tucson to Chicago, I got stuck with a talker. The man had told me jokes and I had slowly grown to hate myself for being the kind of woman who laughs a little too loudly out of politeness at jokes she's heard before that weren't funny the first time. I hadn't quite known this about myself before and resent being forced to learn it now.

When I moved to Tucson ten years ago, my east coast friends were begrudgingly supportive. They swore I'd miss the snow at Christmas, but I haven't. My neighborhood decorates the cactus in their front yards and it's so hilariously tacky and over the top that I finally broke down and joined in, placing a lighted tree on my lawn beside the ocotillo. The first winter I was away, there wasn't as much snow back East. Ally blamed global warming.

"If it gets warm there, I'll move back," I offered. I waited with the phone pressed to my ear and heard nothing. "Don't you care about me more than snow?"

And Ally said: "Well, yeah, but I also care about the world."

I sighed heavily. "Fine."

The east coast is beautiful three months out of the year. The other nine months are gray and cold and miserable. Arizona's exactly the opposite: three months in the summer get a little too hot for comfort. It coincides perfectly for trips east. I've given my winter coat to Goodwill and made it official. I will never see another New

England winter.

The plane lifts off and I have a view of Chicago at night. I've been here several times, but I've never left the airport so I'm unable to recognize any of the buildings. It looks like a quilt with equidistant stitches of light. A ribbon of road glows orange with tail-lights. A patch of so much black must be water.

In the daylight, I was surprised to see how much of the land was still unpopulated. It was a patchwork of greens and browns bordered by empty roads. There was no way to judge the distance this way, no cars to give the area its scale, put it in context.

Ally will pick me up at the airport and she'll be my date for Ethan's wedding. I had thought I might have an actual boyfriend to bring with me this time, but Tim couldn't get the time off. I'm used to being the single girl at weddings. It hardly even bothers me anymore.

Growing up, I had an oak dresser with attached mirror. It was an antique, a family heirloom, and the mirror was original. It was foggy and had a rusty mark shaped like a crescent moon right in the middle. I always had to duck to the side to get a clear impression of myself. I often wished the glass would break so we could replace it with one that had no distortions, but it never did.

It mattered to my mother that the glass was authentic; it increased the value. Not that it would ever be sold. This was a piece of family history to be passed down. As a girl, my mother had folded her bellbottoms and peasant tops into the deep drawers. In its first incarnation, it had belonged to her grandmother, a woman long dead by the time I was born.

As my parents' only child, it went without saying that I'd be the one to inherit the dresser. My mother went further than that, though, assuring me that it would be mine when I got married.

I didn't date in high school, which was probably for the best, really. I had a series of unrequited crushes full of passion and melodrama that never escaped the safety of my seventeen-year-old imagination. My parents didn't meet anyone who fit the criteria of a boyfriend until I was out of college.

Single and preparing a move across the country, I asked my mother what would become of the dresser if I never got married. She blinked and I watched her revise her expectations for my life as easily as shaking an Etch-A-Sketch.

She and my father paid for the moving truck that delivered my belongings. When it arrived, I was so relieved to find the mirror unbroken.

All my girlfriends have managed to marry before their thirtieth birthdays, officially making me the only remaining single girl of the group. I'd always assumed it would work out this way, but it seems to have happened much sooner than I'd expected.

Ally had been the first. She was twenty-three when she announced her engagement and I had to fight the urge to tell her she was too young when the truth was I just wasn't ready.

I came home for Ally's wedding and every summer since. At one point, I thought I might skip a year, but that was the summer Ally ordered a virgin daiquiri at the Mexican restaurant and I did the math. By the following summer, the baby would be three months old.

All of my friends turned out to be the marrying kind, even if they imagined themselves as somewhat unconventional. Each of them had their own way of bucking tradition. Ally had a potluck reception and registered at Unicef. Both of Becca's parents walked her down the aisle. Christine had skipped the bouquet throwing, to my utter relief. This will be my fourth trip home for a wedding and will be only slightly different than the rest: there will be two grooms.

Gay weddings may have become common enough to bore New Yorkers, but they're still a novelty in some parts of the country. They just became legal in Arizona a couple years ago. And we hardly had time to feel superior before the Supreme Court made it the law of the land. Gay marriage bans have suddenly gone the way of laws against inter-racial marriage. Millennials will get to roll their eyes at the idea that it was ever a question, scoff at the way things were in the olden days.

Or so we hope. The new guy in office might just undo everything. The mood was different at Tucson Pride this year. It was still fun, but there was a nervous buzz in the air, more petitions to sign.

Ethan told me about the engagement last summer, when we were still cocky enough to take it for granted as the new normal. I worried he was getting caught up in the politics of it. Just because a thing can be done doesn't mean it should be done.

I met Ethan when we were sophomores at NYU, the year before he dropped out to go traveling in Europe. It's hard to believe we only had that one year together in school before he took off. We stayed in touch through emails and post cards and the telephone. He taught me how to maintain a close connection over distance, a skill that came in handy in the years that followed when the geography of friendship became more and more complicated and I needed to start a life in a city where I knew no one.

One thing I've discovered is that sometimes it's easier to tell the truth in a letter. There are things about me that only Ethan knows.

Since leaving New York, he's lived everywhere. I have post cards from Santa Fe and Barcelona and Miami and there was always a different man that he was following or stumbling upon or running from. His dating history is as diverse as the geography. He and Colin shared an apartment in Boston for three years, the longest he's been in one place since I met him.

"So, what's different about this guy?" I'd asked him.

He looked past me and took a few moments to formulate a response. We were sitting at an outdoor seafood restaurant with iced teas and fried clams. He squinted at the ocean and I worried he was mad at me for asking.

"To be honest," he said, finally, "I'm not sure it's him that's different. I mean, I've dated my fair share of toads over the years, but they weren't all bad. A few nice guys snuck in." He lifted his glass. "But I'm different. I'm ready."

I nodded. I couldn't tell if it was true, but it was comforting that he seemed so sure.

If Tim wanted to get married, I'd marry him. But it isn't important to him and it isn't important enough to me to push it. It's like Christmas at our house. Tim has no Christmas spirit and I have just enough to manage an hour of Christmas carols while I put up the little artificial tree we keep in a cardboard box in the closet. If he thought it was fun, I could get caught up in it, but I don't have the energy to be the leader of the Christmas spirit.

We knew early on that we were the right people for each other, but I'm pretty sure I knew first. When we moved in together, he let me know he was all in. That was five years ago, but it feels like more than that and I don't mean that in a bad way. He's in all my important memories, even things that happened before we met. I just imagine him there.

I brought him home two summers ago and he finally met everyone, got the stamp of approval. Ally called him a keeper; I was already planning on it. This is a man who builds forts for his sixteen-year-old cat. He knows how to let a woman cry without telling her to stop. He's strong enough to hold on and listen.

He tells me he loves the smooth skin of my buttocks; I love the surprisingly soft fur on his chin and the way I can lose my fingers in the jungle of his chest hair. I love the noises he makes when he comes; not the single grunt that I've heard from other men, but a loud animal roar that comes in long bursts as he holds me so tight I think my ribs might crack and I don't even mind; so loud that if we lived in an apartment, the neighbors would complain.

The flight attendant begins taking drink orders and I shake my head. The woman beside me has roused long enough to ask for something I don't catch. Her black hair is coming loose from the large clip. She turns her head and I turn mine as well, looking back out the window to avoid making eye contact.

Outside the clouds are thick, obscuring the darkness below. It resembles a windswept desert with rippled patterns in the sand. Or an infinite, snowy tundra. Or a rumpled bedspread.

I hold a book in my lap and reread the praise on the back cover. I lean my head against the window and find a cloud that resembles the Titanic. I glance at my watch.

A woman is standing in the aisle, waiting for the restroom in spite of a sign instructing against this. Since 9/11, there are announcements at the beginning of the flight. Your seat can be used as a flotation device and don't stand near the cockpit door. The sign is right there in bold letters and the woman is practically touching it.

I haven't had to use an airplane restroom in years, a feat I accomplish only by the refusal of the drinks offered, seemingly on the hour, during the flight. They don't feed passengers anymore, but they sure do hydrate them.

The plane dips and we're inside the clouds. Illuminated by the airplane lights, the bright white presses against my window. Nearing the airport, I see the scattered, disorganized lights of New Hampshire – so different from the geometry of Chicago.

The woman beside me leans forward to share the view. "Are you flying home or are you on vacation?"

Both, I think. "I grew up here."

"Are you coming from Chicago?"

"Tucson."

"What brought you to Tucson?"

"The weather."

"What do you do?"

"I don't work."

"What does your husband do?"

"I'm not married." I hold out my left hand with its naked ring finger and allow for the inevitable awkward pause. I'm learning to feel comfortable with awkward pauses.

Tim and I are agreed on not having children. It's more than just wanting time for other things, feeling like the world is overcrowded enough, having no desire to perpetuate your genetics – I mean, it's all those things. And I don't want the most significant thing I do with my life to be creating another. It seems like a never-ending way of passing the buck.

I've heard about the biological clock, but so far, mine is silent. Pregnancy sounds like torture: a parasite taking over your insides. No, thank you.

When Ally was pregnant, I had managed to find it beautiful, even miraculous. I had known other people who'd had babies, had about a dozen baby cousins, but somehow Lucy seemed like the first baby. Ever. That Ally had created another human being was absolutely unbelievable. And yet, there she was, the proof in her pretty blue eyes, an exact duplicate of her mother's. Pools of blue with pebbles at the bottom. "She stole your eyeballs," I said when we met for the first time. I held Lucy in the crook of my arm and let her suck my pinky. I looked up nervously. "Is this allowed?"

Already over the germ phobia of new motherhood, and totally at ease, Ally just laughed.

Part of coming to terms with the idea that the human race is on its way out is not having children who will have to live through the apocalypse. Unfortunately, I have begun to realize there's a flaw in the plan when you have friends on the mommy track: you still have to care about the future.

The seatbelt sign bleeps off overhead and the plane is filled with the clicking of impatient passengers. Most of them stand before they're supposed to. I finish the paragraph of the book I've been trying to read and slide my bookmark into place.

People fill the aisles, yanking bags out of the overhead bins. I sigh, closing my book and leaning forward. I rub my neck and roll my shoulders. I peer out the window at the tiny blinking lights along the runway. I watch as another plane lifts off and disappears from view.

The woman who was sitting next to me takes a step back and motions with her arm, suggesting I should step in front of her.

"Oh, thanks, go ahead. I'm not ready," I say.

The woman tilts her head in confusion. Her fellow passengers are eager to leave though, so she's forced to move along.

When the aisle has cleared, even the stragglers, those haggard passengers traveling with children and diaper bags and strollers, a flight attendant returns my things to me.

The porter pushes my wheelchair to the front of the aisle. I stand and maneuver my way into the seat. There's some small talk on the trip up the jetway before I can take over the driving.

"Thanks. I got it from here," I say over my shoulder. I find my cell phone inside the pocket of my tiny purse and I send a text message to Ally: *Here*.

Ally: Tuesday

The girls are in the tub when I leave. Karl sits on the toilet in our too-small bathroom, barely room for a person to stand between the toilet and the sink. I hear Grace's high-pitched shriek as I start down the stairs. Over the phone, Sara can never tell if it's a happy screech or a mad screech, always halting her storytelling in case I have to drop the phone and scoop Grace up.

I continue down the stairs, secure in the knowledge that it is a happy screech. She's probably spilling water out of her yellow cup or grabbing the rubber frog away from her sister. I'm on the second-floor landing when I hear the mad screech. Lucy must have taken exception, grabbed it back. She knows better than to hit. She outgrew hitting before Grace came along. Good news for Grace; not soon enough to spare me. I once shut myself in the bathroom to escape one of her hitting fits. Everyone warned me about the terrible twos, but for us it was terrible threes. Grace came along just after Lucy's fourth birthday and things had actually gotten easier. A potty-trained four-year-old and a newborn are a breeze compared to the chaos of a single toddler.

In the driveway, I remember all over again that we're sharing Karl's beater now. The SUV was repossessed three days ago and other than the inconvenience of car seat retrieval, I'm feeling the loss of the car payment looming over our heads and counting it as a relief.

Sliding into the driver's seat, I remember one of the downsides: it smells like an ash tray. Karl isn't allowed to smoke in my car, or in sight of the girls, but we made no such rule about this $500 piece of shit that was intended to be the "extra" car, just meant to get Karl back and forth to work. I roll down the window for the drive to the airport and hope Sara won't notice.

I haven't seen her since last summer. Grace was three weeks old. That whole week is a blur and I only know it's real because there are photos.

I'm sitting upstairs in the airport when she texts me that she's landed. I wait as the rest of the travelers flood through security, knowing she'll be last. When she comes through, she looks tired, but when she sees me, her face lights up. She's always known how to rally.

"I already peed," she says as she hugs me around the neck.

"Hungry?"

"Starving."

By the time we get to baggage, all the carousels have stopped. Her little black duffel bag is sitting off to the side. It must be easy to pack light when your clothes are as tiny as hers are. I heft the bag over my hip and we head to the parking garage. She pouts at the car. I told her what happened over the phone, in tears, days ago.

"I've come to terms," I explain as she sets the brake on her wheelchair and feels for the handle on the ceiling. She liked the SUV. It was the perfect height for her to climb into. Whenever she stands, I'm surprised all over again by how tall she is. This car sits lower and it takes her a couple minutes to figure out how to fold herself inside.

When she does, she smiles. "Tada!"

At the gate, I pull the parking ticket from beneath the visor and Sara groans. "I used up my cash before I left."

"That's okay," I say quickly, rifling through my wallet. It's thick with baby photos and receipts and coupons. But money?

"Four dollars," says the woman at the gate.

I find three in the wallet and toss it aside. I run my hand along the pocket in the door, check the visor again.

"You're in luck," I say, finding the fourth dollar bill in the center console. She doesn't have the gall to point out that I'm the one in luck. I had nearly been forced into bartering to get out of the parking garage. *Here's three dollars and my daughter's half-empty sippy cup. Do we have a deal?*

"I'm buying dinner," Sara says. "I've got my credit card."

We go to the place we like with the brick oven pizza and the roasted vegetables. It's quieter than usual, since it's a Monday and it's nearly ten o'clock. We talk about Tim and the girls and Sara's parents and my nursing classes.

I tell her about Karl's grandparents, how they've just realized Grammy has Alzheimer's. She was the one taking care of Grampa, who's been sick for years. Now they have twenty-four-hour care in their house. They have too much money to qualify for state aid, but at this rate they'll go through their savings within the year.

"Grammy has asked us to move in."

Sara lifts her eyebrows and chews.

"We'd be able to help each other, really. I mean, Karl and I wouldn't have to pay rent and they wouldn't have to pay for constant nursing care or move into a home."

"That would be a lot of work, though, wouldn't it?"

"I know. But I'm used to hard work. It wouldn't be anything I haven't done before."

"That's true. It might be easier. Less lifting."

I nod. I used to work in a nursing home. I'd loved that job, but had to quit because of the back strain.

Sara puts down her fork and picks up the crust with her hands. "You'd never really have time to yourself though, but I'm not sure how much of that you get as it is with two kids."

"No, I sure don't." I laugh. "I think it might be good for me. It would make me feel like I was doing something meaningful with my life."

"Besides raising two amazing kids?"

I smile. "Yeah. Besides that." She's always quick to remind me of this. I know being a mom is an important job. But I started working when I was fourteen, picking trash at the beach, the only job I could find that hired workers under sixteen. Before the girls came along, I'd worked full-time since I was seventeen years old. In fact, I worked eighteen-hour days at the bakery, on my feet, up until two days before Lucy was born. Now it was all on Karl to pay the bills: the rent, the car, the phone, the groceries, preschool. And every month we had to pick which ones to pay. "It's just hard. It would make me feel like I was contributing."

She opens her mouth to argue.

"In a more... concrete way."

She nods. "Okay. I can see that."

"It's sort of nice. Karl has always felt like a bit of an outcast in his family, but they didn't ask any of the other siblings. They trusted him with this."

The waiter comes to ask if we want to see the dessert menu. We look at each other. "Well, we should take a look at the menu, at least," Sara tells the waiter and I nod in agreement.

"Karl's family has just castrated him." I continue when he leaves. I pause, twist my mouth to the side. "No. That's not the right word."

She's laughing. "Karl will love that you're telling people he's been castrated. I don't believe it, though. You've had two of his babies."

"I was trying to say that they act like he's the black sheep. What's the word I meant?"

Still laughing, she leans forward to sip her water through the straw, without raising the heavy glass. "Um . . . I'm not sure. Castigate?"

I don't think that's it either, but it doesn't matter. Sara knows what I mean.

The waiter returns with the list of desserts. We decide to share something and the negotiations are delicate. I try to figure out what she wants; she tries to figure out what I want. We end up choosing the cheesecake, which is probably not what either of us want.

"Well, that's huge," she pronounces after the waiter takes our order. "It sounds like it could be perfect timing. A Godsend."

It's a funny choice of words coming from her. Sara's belief in God is tenuous, as far as I know.

I drop Sara at the hotel, the one she always stays at since her parents moved to Florida years ago. She loves it because she knows it will really be handicap accessible, unlike so many hotels in New England. I love it because it's closer to my house than the seaside town where we grew up.

As it is, it's after midnight when I trudge back up those stairs.

Karl's asleep in the living room when I get home. I turn off the television. This is how most of our days end: one of us coming home to find the other asleep. When Karl gets home from his second job cleaning carpets for his dad's business, he'll try to wake me. I usually curse at him and have no memory of it in the morning. He'll give up and I'll wake at 3 AM, putting myself to bed.

Tonight, he wakes when I snap off the television. He stretches. "Bedtime, Bubba."

He nods. His eyes are cloudy. Part of him is still dreaming.

"Did the girls go to bed good?"

He grips the arms of the chair and pulls himself to his feet with a groan. "Lucy made me read the same story three times."

"Lila the Ladybug?" I kick off my shoes.

"Yeah."

"That's her new favorite."

"I miss Green Eggs and Ham."

"Maybe she'll cycle back."

Karl climbs into bed next to me and we fidget over the covers.

"I haven't had time to read a book in about a year," he says.

"A year?" I'm amused. It's like he's trying to impress me with his literary-ness. Ten years married and he's acting like we're on a first date, like I don't *know* him. "And what book was that, honey?"

He squints at the ceiling, scratches his chin. "That one about the war?"

"World War II?"

"Yeah."

"Yeah, you read that while I was pregnant with Lucy. She's five, dummy. Nice try."

He grumbles a half-hearted protest. If he wasn't so tired, he'd argue with me. As it is, he rolls over, taking a good bit of the duvet with him. I tug it back and settle into my pillow.

I give him a hard time, but he's a good man. Last week, when I was studying for my nursing exam, he stripped down and let me cover him with sticky notes, labeling his muscles and organs and bones. The kids were in bed and he was tired from his second job and he stood there in the kitchen in his underwear and I thought: *this man really loves me.*

We were more than five years in before we had our first hiccup, beyond his constant forgetting to take out the trash.

There was a woman. He didn't sleep with her. That's what he said and I believe him. If I didn't believe him, he'd be dead and I'd be in prison and Lucy would be in foster care. And Grace wouldn't exist.

Yeah, I'd kill him with my bare hands if he did that to me. That's the kind of woman I am. Divorce is for other people.

The woman's name was *Lisa*. Every time I think of her, that's how I hear her name. With a lilt and a sneer. She was a friend of his from work who I'd never met. She was going through a divorce and just needed someone to talk to. So, he was listening. And talking, too. About our marital problems, the ones I didn't know we were having. Instead of talking to me. Or listening to me. His wife.

She'd call him and text him when he was home. He'd say it was one of his guy friends, but I knew. I knew because of the way he'd shove the phone into his pocket so quickly after checking it.

I also knew because I went through his phone while he was in the shower. When he got out, I'd dumped his entire wardrobe over the balcony in the snow.

He claimed he only lied to keep me from freaking out. He promised to tell her she had to stop calling. In the wee hours of the morning, wearing my purple bathrobe, he picked his clothes off the snowy lawn.

I was driving us home from my parent's house one night when his cell phone chimed and he looked at it and quickly shoved it back in his pocket.

"Who was that?"

"Doug." It was a small comfort that he was such a lousy liar.

"Oh, yeah? What did Doug want?"

"Nothing. Just work stuff."

"Don't lie to me."

"I'm not. It was Doug."

I pulled the car into a parking lot we were about to drive past. "Give me your phone."

"No."

"Give it to me!" Lucy had been dozing in the backseat, but the combination of the car coming to a stop and my screaming unsettled her. She rubbed her face without opening her eyes. Karl sat with his arms folded, not looking at me.

"We will stay in this car all night," I hissed. "Give me your phone."

Lucy whimpered uncertainly in her half sleep. Karl seemed to be weighing his options.

"Fine." He dug into his pocket and threw the phone at me. The text was from Doug. I felt a mixture of relief and embarrassment. I was the irrational, jealous wife.

But then I looked closer. *OMG*, the text said. *PLZ tell me u work 2morrow.* Doug didn't talk like that. And it wasn't his number. It was his name, but it was her number.

I got out of the car. I was tearing at my hands, trying to get my rings off.

Karl got out and ran around the side of the car toward me.

"Stay away from me!" I warned him. "You changed her name in your cell phone so she could call and I wouldn't know!"

The parking lot was nearly empty.

"I'm not sleeping with her, Ally! I swear to God!"

"Then why is she so important to you?"

"She's my friend."

"No." I shook my finger at him. "If she was your friend, she'd come to the house for dinner to meet your wife, instead of sneaking around and communicating in secret."

"We aren't sneaking around!"

"What do you call this?" I screamed, throwing the cell phone at him. It hit his shoulder and flew past him, landing on the pavement and breaking in pieces.

"It's not what you think."

It was such a cliché that I just screamed up at the night sky and began tugging at my rings again.

"I didn't know how to tell her not to call me. It makes me sound like a child. Are you my *mother*?"

The edge in his voice enraged me. As if he felt he had the right to be angry. "No, I'm not your fucking mother! I'm the mother of your child! The child I'm going to take with me when I leave you for cheating on me!" And, with that, my rings came loose and I flung them away from me, into the dark.

"Ally, what are you doing?" He started crying. "I swear to God, Ally, I would never cheat on you." He got down on his hands and knees in the dark, searching.

We'd saved up for months to buy those rings. A modest diamond in platinum and a band that matched his, inscribed with lyrics from our wedding song.

I imagined taking Lucy to Tucson to live with Sara. Karl would never see either of us ever again.

And then I heard her, wailing, on the other side of the window. I yanked open the door and unhooked her from the car seat. We climbed into the front of the car and I rocked her, murmuring that everything would be okay.

Karl searched that parking lot for two hours. Lucy fell asleep in my arms and I returned her to the backseat. She was so beautiful and innocent, dependent on us to keep her safe and happy. I found Karl in the darkness, pulled him to his feet and made him drive us home. He'd only managed to find my engagement ring.

Sara's the only person who knows about that night. Just after that, Lucy started having nightmares and I was sure that was the cause. Sara tried to tell me I was being too hard on myself. "Sometimes kids just have nightmares, right?" And when I remained unconvinced, she suggested Karl and I should try couples counseling. As if I could afford that. Sara had gone to therapy after college and now she thinks it's something normal people do.

Eventually, Lucy went back to sleeping through the night and things with Karl got good again. Hard to say which came first.

In the morning, Lucy climbs into our bed at 5 AM. She pushes her little body in between us. After an hour of half-dozing while she wriggles around, I shake Karl and he gets up and carries her back to her room. Grace starts fussing a half hour later and I give up.

Karl comes into the kitchen wearing boxers and a t-shirt while I'm distributing orange slices and sippy cups.

"I talked to my mom last night," he says, rubbing his disheveled hair. "They want to start the trial week tomorrow."

"Tomorrow? But Sara's here this week. We have the wedding on Saturday."

"That's fine. I'll be home with the girls just like we planned. The point is to see how it would work with us living our normal life."

"You're sure you want this?"

"I think so. If it works for you and the girls. I know it could be hard on them."

To be honest, I'm more worried about him. At the nursing home, I've seen Alzheimer's up close. It's a cruel disease. The body lasts and lasts, long after the mind is gone. It's the most heartbreaking for the people who are forgotten. "I think the girls are too small to have expectations. But are you prepared? Eventually, she'll look you right in the eye and have no clue who you are."

He sits at the table and strokes Grace's head. She brushes him off, intent on chasing the Cheerios across the tray on her high chair. "When I was in high school, I lived with them for a summer."

I know the story, but I let him tell it again because he needs to.

At sixteen, he was butting heads with his father, staying out all night and running around with kids he admits were the wrong crowd. His parents didn't know what to do so they sent him to Grammy and Grampa who lived in a small town, far enough away from his new friends to keep him out of trouble. He didn't talk back to his grandparents and he didn't refuse when they asked him to help mow the lawn or core apples. "How could I fight with a woman who had arthritic fingers and just wanted to feed me pie?"

"You feel like you owe them?"

"It's not about owing," he says, almost angrily. "Who knows where I'd be if they hadn't stepped up? Those guys I was hanging around with never amounted to much. One of them died in a knife fight before we were out of high school."

"That's awful." When I met Karl, we were in our early twenties. He was a manager at the hardware store in the same plaza as the restaurant where I waitressed. He used to come in for lunch. If not for that job, we might never have met.

"They were there for me at a hard time and I want to be there for them in their hard time. That's what family means."

This is why I married him. These are the lessons I want my girls to learn. I wrap my arms around him, around the boy he was and the man he's become.

Delilah: Wednesday

I'm afraid to use my credit card. I don't like to admit it, even to myself, but I'm running out of cash.

Phrases pass through my mind, things like *paper trail* and *metadata,* and I find myself googling out-of-state arrest warrants, reading about extradition policies.

Not that I know for sure that there is a warrant, but there was that cop car. Something I read says that a warrant will follow you *to the grave.* Years will pass and you'll get pulled over for something minor and end up getting arrested.

I cut to the chase. In the cool silence of the guest bedroom, I huddle over my laptop and type: *How do I find out if there's an arrest warrant in my name?* I hit send and hold my breath. Several links come up in the search. I type in my name, the state I'm looking in. There aren't many Delilahs in New Hampshire, only one Delilah Jane Wilkins, thirty-three years old. It shows all my former addresses. I click the green button to compile the report and the horizontal status bar fills slowly. It promises personal information and police records and former roommates and lists of property I own (that'll be short). I wait and it blinks to the next page where I'm asked to sign in, supply my credit card, and pay $22.87.

I slam the laptop shut and hop off the bed. It's so quiet with Sadie at school and David at work, seems like a waste. I imagine the neighborhood full of big empty houses cranking out air conditioning for no one. Perhaps one or two of them have a retiree or a stay-at-home mom. (Do they still have those? Maybe they do in a neighborhood as nice as this one.)

And then there's me, of course. Whatever I am. The loser little sister, hiding out, *on the lam.*

David thinks a man hit me, lil' ol' defenseless me. Some big brute with no right. I can never tell him it was a willowy blond girl who took exception to me vandalizing her car.

Who does that? I've never done anything like it my entire life. They'll take that into consideration when sentencing, I'm sure.

They'll go easy on the former social worker who lost her damn mind.

I go out to the backyard and lay on a lounge chair. David has left money and a grocery list on the kitchen counter. I'll go later; I volunteered. For now, I doze in the late morning sun, pretending I'm on a resort vacation instead of possibly *on the run* from the police.

My cell phone chirps. Leslie again. She's left two messages I haven't returned. The first one sounded worried; the second was mad. The email I sent on Sunday had been too vague. I told her things with Marty were over and I'd gone away to think.

The text she sends now reads: *Where are you???*

Her frustration can be measured by the number of question marks.

I'm afraid to answer. What if the police ask her? She hasn't mentioned the police. She hasn't mentioned talking to Marty either and I can only hope she doesn't. If he tells her what I did, she'll be horrified.

I'm horrified.

I drive the speed limit on the way to the grocery store, use my blinker properly at all the turns. I've added an item to David's list: aloe. I fell asleep in the sun and now my skin feels tightly stretched across my body and I'm aware of it in a way that makes me realize how infrequently I think of my skin. I shiver in the air conditioning and hurry through the frozen food section. Most of what I need is in produce. Limes and cilantro and onions for the chili.

There are so many different kinds of green peppers, not just bell and jalepeno. There's Serrano and Poblana and Anaheim and Pasilla. I took Spanish in high school and in spite of my own horrible accent, I know the way the words are meant to sound. The double Ls stand in for a Y. The Js sound like Hs. The language is rolling and lyrical and I pause in several aisles, pretending to scan the shelves, just so I can hear it spoken. I have no idea what they're saying, but it doesn't matter.

It turns out the peppers I need for the chili come in a can, along with the green enchilada sauce and the beans. I choose the ones labeled mild.

I pick a line that's moving quickly and pile my items onto the conveyor belt. The cashier looks up at me and gasps. "Oh, honey, you're not from around here, are you?"

I try to laugh, but it feels like it might split the hot pink sausage casing that is my face. "It's my first time here," I admit. It's my first time anywhere, really. Other than a weekend at the Cape with Leslie, where have I ever been? "In New England, I've only gotten a tan if I was out at high noon without sunscreen."

She raises her eyebrows and shakes her head like this is unimaginable. "SPF 40 is your friend," she says, nodding approval at the aloe. "And a hat."

I pass her David's twenty; she hands me my receipt. "I'm hoping it browns up," I say, considering the color of my forearm.

She laughs. "Just pray it doesn't blister." And when I've gathered my purchases to leave, she calls out to me: "Be careful."

I promise that I will.

In the beginning, dating an addict was sort of thrilling. Marty didn't feel the need to drink because whatever alcohol had done to even out his brain chemistry, falling in love with me was just as good.

At first.

It felt like such a compliment, to replace the thing that stimulated the pleasure centers in his brain. I remember feeling as if I'd cured him, had filled the gaping wound inside that made him think he needed alcohol. It turned out, all he really needed was me. I was his drug of choice.

We had sex constantly and we spent the first nine months talking about how amazing we felt, how lucky we were to have found each other. The first time he went out with the boys, it didn't even occur to me to worry. At 1 AM, his buddy called me on his cell phone because Marty was too drunk to be understood, never mind drive. I picked him up that night and we went back for his car the next afternoon. I was so angry we hardly spoke that first time, but it became routine; that was just what we did on Saturday.

Marty never remembered the drive home from the bar or anything much after his twelfth beer. He didn't remember me undressing him or cleaning the vomit and he didn't remember the snippets of slurred stories he told about his dad.

The thing it took me time to realize is that it wasn't me that replaced the drug. It was the act of falling in love. It was the sex and gushing conversation about how good we had it. That was the high.

It never had anything to do with me.

There's only one way to know.

I hold the cell phone in my shaking hand and select his number.

I put it down on the counter and take a step back as if it's a live creature, something venomous and suited to my new surroundings. A black widow spider.

I switch on the stove and walk to the refrigerator. Ground turkey. A little jar of minced garlic. I put the pot on the burner and look at the clock. It's just past four but it feels later. David's picking Sadie up from an after school thing, something dorky and responsible like science club. Part of me hopes she's really making out with her boyfriend under the bleachers, but maybe she's really as well-behaved as she appears. I was at her age. The boundaries testing came later. It always comes eventually.

At any rate, I'll have the house to myself for the next hour at least. I dump the turkey into the pot and pick up the phone. It rings in the crook of my neck as I toss in the garlic and break up the meat with a spatula. It rings four times and I think about hanging up.

Instead, he answers. It hurts to hear him say my name. "Where the hell are you?"

I sigh. I didn't call to answer his questions. "None of your business. I need you to tell me something."

"You need *me* to tell *you* something?" he asks, incredulous. "It's been over a week! I need you to tell me where you are."

"Why? Why do you care?" It's not as if he has called me. I didn't change my number. Perhaps his new woman checks his call log. That would be smart. *If he'll do it with you, he'll do it to you.* It would serve her right to spend their entire relationship paranoid and insecure. *You reap what you sow.*

"Of course I care about you," he says.

"You *care* about me? Fuck you."

The turkey begins to smoke. I turn down the temperature.

"You have every right to be angry," he says and for some reason I start laughing. "But you haven't heard my side!"

"Your side?" I roll my eyes even though he can't see me. He's probably sitting on his couch with the television on mute. He stomps one foot like a little boy when he thinks what he's saying is important.

"It's not like I planned it. At first, I thought it was just a one time slip. But then I really fell for her and—"

"I do *not* want to hear about your tragic love story." This is definitely not why I called –to contemplate what a struggle he's been through these last months as I lost my job and interviewed for positions I was overqualified for and cut down my monthly budget so much that I was thrilled to be hired anywhere. And while I was working weekends and gratefully taking overtime, he was trying so so hard (and failing) not to fall in love with some leggy blond bitch.

"Okay, but things had been bad with us for a while. And you were so down."

"What the hell does that mean?" I bring the cans to the electric can opener and shout over the whirring. "You cheated on me 'cuz I wasn't upbeat enough?"

"No. I just. I didn't know how to tell you." He pauses. "I thought you might hurt yourself," he says quietly.

"Oh, shut up." I throw the beans in the pot. "Stop trying to paint a picture of yourself as the big hero protecting me from the truth. You're a coward, that's all."

I stomp back to the fridge and rummage in the vegetable drawer. He wants me to forgive him, to see him as the good guy in all this. I dismiss the idea that there's even a kernel of truth here, but it does weigh on me: the idea that he's convinced himself that I was so fragile. This comes from the person who should have known me best.

"I know I did the wrong thing," he says. "I know I handled it badly. I need you to know that I know these things."

I'm so tired of hearing about what he needs. "I don't care about any of this," I say and I'm surprised to realize this feels, at least for the moment, mostly true. I lay the veggies on a cutting board and slide a knife from the drawer, one of those super sharp knives that real chefs have. I pin the phone between my left ear and shoulder. "I want to know if there's a—" Suddenly I'm not sure how to say it. "If I need to be worried about—"

"STDs?"

I cut the onion in half with the big, fancy knife. "No!" Though suddenly, my mind is racing. Should I be worried about that? The scent of onion stings my eyes. It had been months since we'd made love. It had worried me at first – so unusual for us. But then I dismissed it. Our work schedules were out of sync. It was normal to have lulls in a long term relationship. I plow ahead. "Is there a warrant?"

"A warrant?"

"For what I did to her car." I remember the sound of glass raining on asphalt, the pressure of his hand between my shoulders, pushing me.

"That was pretty fucked up, Li."

"Marty!" I drop the knife and step away, not trusting myself to pay close enough attention. I rub my eyes with the back of my hand, but that only makes it worse.

"No, there's not a warrant. Jesus."

"There was a police cruiser at my apartment that night." I lean against the counter with my eyes squeezed shut.

"Well, we called the cops but she didn't press charges."

When the tears start streaming down my face, I blame the onion, but that doesn't explain why I can't catch my breath to speak or why my knees buckle and I collapse to the floor and start sobbing. I can still hear him talking when I hang up.

At dinner, they're all adding hot sauce and I'm drinking too much wine and trying to stop sweating.

"I learned how to eat real Mexican food when I went away to college in California," David says. "New Hampshire's Mexican is not the same."

I scowl. "So, you're saying I can't help it."

"It's an adjustment."

"I grew up drinking salsa from a bottle," Sadie boasts, licking her fingers.

"I don't think Sara ever adjusted." Tim's sitting across from me, dipping his bread. "She's from Massachusetts, so, basically New Hampshire."

I pretend to double over as if I've been stabbed, clutching my stomach. "That's so insulting! Massachusetts is an armpit. It's nothing like New Hampshire."

Tim laughs and David makes a face and I realize this is an old joke between them.

"You must be used to all kinds of different foods," I say to Tim. "David told me you drove your motorcycle around the world."

Tim nods, chews. We wait. "Nothing's spicier than Mexican."

"You didn't go through Thailand," David reminds him.

I turn to him, accusatory. "You've been to Thailand?"

"Honeymoon," he says, and it begins to sound vaguely familiar. I remember a photo of David and Janet on a rickshaw, laughing. I never knew what changed between them.

I reach for the wine bottle and refill my glass. "And what about you?" I say, pointing at Sadie.

"What about me?" She feigns an attitude, but I can tell she's glad to be included.

"Where's the furthest you've been?"

She pauses to think it over, dragging it out. "Costa Rica on a school trip."

I groan. "I've never been anywhere except that one time my parents took me to Disney World when I was nine."

David turns to me, looking wounded. "They took you to Disney World?"

I nod.

"What did you do there?"

I can hardly remember. It was sunny and humid and my hair was a big ball of frizz all week. "Ate too many sweets, rode rollercoasters."

"By yourself?"

"No. With mom and dad."

He looks appalled by this. "*Rollercoasters?*"

I nod and he says the word again and shakes his head. Sadie giggles like his confusion is funny, but I can't help thinking what different childhoods we managed to have with the same parents. It isn't fair his was so much harder. I can't imagine it. Truth is, I don't want to.

I look across the table at Tim. "What made you do it? Just drop everything and go?"

Tim looks up from his bowl, startled, like he hadn't expected to be the center of attention. He wipes his mouth with a paper napkin and sits back in his chair. "People are always putting things off," he says. "My mother had all these big plans for her retirement. She was going to go to Europe. She was going to see the ocean. She wanted to attend a Mardis Gras." He sighs. "Instead she got cancer and died at forty."

My breath catches and I reach for his hand. The gesture is too intimate and I'm glad he's sitting beyond my grasp. "I'm so sorry," I say, and my hand flits awkwardly, aimlessly, and I pretend I was getting another slice of bread. "I lost my mother, too." I motion to David, remembering. "Our mother."

"He took some amazing pictures on his trip," David says.

"Oh, I'd love to see them sometime."

"They're up on my blog." Tim reaches in his back pocket and pulls out his wallet. His hands are big and worn, but his fingers are long and graceful. He flips open the billfold and slides out a card. "Sara made these."

Sara. The girlfriend.

He pushes the card across the table to me and I take it. It's a photo of a motorcycle on the roadside. I've never been on a motorcycle either. How have I managed to live such a sheltered life?

"That's what you should do, Sadie!" I slap the table and Sadie tips her head at me. "Not on a motorcycle, but you should travel. When you graduate."

"What about college?"

I wave my hand in the air. "What's the rush?" I hold Tim's card between my thumb and first finger. It's warm and smooth. The font is sans serif. His name, his email, a website. His phone number. "Besides, is this really the best time to be gambling that a college education will even make you employable in this economy?"

Sadie sits back. Her bowl is empty.

"I never finished college," Tim says. "My employer hired me because I could do the job. I didn't need to pay for a piece of paper that said I could do the job."

"What do you do?" I ask. I remember him in his motorcycle gear.

"I'm a computer programmer."

It's not what I expect. I don't really know what a programmer does, but anything involving computers conjures up someone scrawny and pale, bespectacled. Tim is none of these things.

"A college degree has only become more necessary in this economy," David insists.

"There are a lot of jobs you don't need a degree for." I say.

Tim leans forward, nodding emphatically. "Sara has a friend who is this amazing cake decorator, but fancy bakeries want her to have a culinary degree. They want her to go to school and pay to learn to do something she already knows how to do."

"It's crazy," I agree.

"Yeah, well." David crosses his arms. "Sadie wants to be a doctor."

Tim and I start laughing.

"Well, I guess you do need a degree for that," I say.

Sadie smiles quietly and I realize she hasn't chimed in for this part of the conversation. I remember our talk at Starbucks on Saturday, when she told me she didn't know what she wanted to be when she grew up. Perhaps this doctor thing is just an answer Sadie gave to David once when she was a kid and he held onto it.

Tim is still chuckling. His hair is a golden brown; only his beard is streaked with silver. I've never kissed a man with facial hair. The list of things I've never done seems endless. I push my wine glass away.

It occurs to me that now I can go back to New Hampshire if I want to. What's waiting for me there besides a crappy apartment and a good frying pan?

And that's when I remember Leslie. I forgot to text her after I talked to Marty and it's too late now. I'll email her before I go to bed. I'll tell her I'm in Tucson with my big brother and I'm going to be okay.

It doesn't matter that I'm not sure it's true.

Ally: Thursday

Grammy shuffles into the kitchen while I'm making lunch. "I don't think this will work," she says. "The kids are so busy."

She struggles to pull the chair out from the kitchen table. I wipe my hands on a towel and pull it out for her. She sits down and I sit across from her.

"Okay, well that's fine," I say. I look past her, out the doorway. Lucy is singing and dancing in front of the television set. Grace is playing with her blocks. This is our version of calm and tranquil. "I know this isn't what you're used to. That's why we're doing this trial week. There are other options. You and Grampa can go live with Donna and Paul."

Grammy shakes her head. "He's not really our cup of tea."

I suppress a smile. He isn't anyone's cup of tea. Unfortunately, Donna's the only one of her children to offer. Their eldest son lives so far away. Karl's parents had downsized just last year; they don't have room.

"Well, it's up to you, Gram. But you can't afford to keep having the in-home nurses so we have to figure something out."

She nods and pats my hand. "I'm going to go lay down," she says and she flattens her wrinkled hands against the table and pushes herself to her feet.

I continue making the sandwiches, thinking of all the ways it will be easier for us to stay where we are. We won't need to pack or sort through the storage in the basement. Lucy won't have to change kindergartens. She's already made friends.

I'm strapping Grace into her booster seat when Grammy comes back in.

"That was a quick nap."

She pats Grace's head. "I was thinking about it and I think you should move in here."

"Oh, yeah?" This is how Alzheimer's is in the beginning. Mildly amusing.

She opens the door of the refrigerator and pulls out three cans of ginger ale, setting them in a row along the counter. "You could help us out and we could help you out. I know how you kids are struggling. Grampa and I wouldn't have to leave our house."

"Well, you think about it. If that's what you want, we can make it happen."

When I turn back to the sandwiches, Grammy tries to shoo me away, but I insist I'm on a roll. She takes a plate out to Grampa who sits in the recliner in the living room, dozing and pretending to read the paper. I've been keeping a low-key eye on him, checking for signs of dementia. He's so quiet, it's hard to tell, but I noticed the crossword was mostly finished and his answers didn't seem to be gibberish.

For the last several years, he was the one we'd worried about. He has diabetes and limited mobility from having a foot amputated. Grammy cared for him. More recently, we noticed he was the one reminding about pills, about schedules. They were caring for each other, complementary halves to a whole.

Grammy comes back in and takes a seat at the kitchen table. I call Lucy in from the other room. Her show isn't over; she whines for five more minutes. I march in and turn off the TV myself. "Lunch," I say and I use the voice that means there'll be no negotiation.

She sulks over her sandwich, but sulking I can handle. Sulking is quiet and punishes no one. Last summer, she had a meltdown in the parking lot after a perfectly pleasant lunch with Sara. She was screeching and pulling away from me and lying on the pavement. I had to pick her up and force her wriggling body into the car seat. When I told her to stop being a naughty girl, she shrieked: "I am not a naughty girl!" It was blood curdling and managed to shame me.

"I know you're not a naughty girl, but you're being naughty right now," I said carefully, painfully aware of the trauma I might be inflicting. I struggled to get her buckled in as her body contorted and she cried. When I finally finished, I carried a sleeping Grace to the other side of the car to buckle her in as well. By the time I climbed behind the wheel, I was breathless and disheveled.

Beside me, Sara asked quietly: "Why is Lucy saying she doesn't want a shot?" and I had to admit my ultimate parenting failure: I'd threatened her with a trip to the doctor if she didn't stop.

That was a bad day. We haven't had one of those for a while and I want to believe we might make it through the week without such a display, but I feel myself bristle each time she doesn't get her way on something. If she knew the power she had over me, I'd be in real trouble.

"Have you told your parents?" Sara asks, zipping her fleece up to her chin in the late afternoon sun.

Grace sits in the sand pit at our feet. Lucy waves from the swing set across the park. Sara and I wave back and she continues to swing contentedly.

"Nope and I don't plan to until it's definite." I shake my head. "I can already hear my mom. I'm not telling her until after the decision is made, until it's final."

Sara nods. She remembers what a hard time my mother gave me when I moved to New Hampshire just after I got married. She acted like it was a move across the country, a betrayal. She swore she'd never visit and all these years later she still acts like the "city" roads in Manchester confuse her. She only comes if my father drives.

"Grammy and Grampa's house isn't that much further away. It actually takes about the same amount of time to drive here from the coast as it will if we move. Maybe ten more minutes. But I know it'll be another cause for hysteria."

A young mother enters the park with her son perched on her hip, a large diaper bag hanging from the opposite shoulder. He looks to be about a year old, with copper hair like his mother's. She smiles at me and sets him down at the opposite end of the sand box. He spits out his pacifier and she quickly exchanges it for another in the bag, then pulls out a sand pail and several different colored shovels. Grace looks up at me and I feel an accusation. She's been using her hands. It's only when she sees the shovels that she seems dissatisfied.

"What about your dad?" Sara asks. Her light brown bangs fall in her eyes and she blows them off her forehead with a grimace.

"Oh, you know my dad. He's always supportive. If I asked him to, he'd remove each of his teeth, one by one with a set of pliers."

"Yeah, you got him wrapped around your finger at an early age."

Sara and I have known each other since we were fourteen. We went to high school together in a small town in Massachusetts. I remember the house she grew up in and she remembers the one-sided infatuation that consumed all my years in high school. I knew her when she was still walking and she knew me when I was still thin. We made matching fairy costumes one Halloween with a little felt, some hot glue, and a lot of glitter. We got drunk on wine coolers and raced our cars on back roads (though, not in that order.) Even looking back with the changed perspective of a parent, we were mostly good kids.

"Karl's the same with our girls," I say. "I know I'll always have to be the disciplinarian. He's too smitten."

"I love that."

I roll my eyes. Truth is, I love it too. Mostly.

"A few years ago, Tim's single dad friend went to see The Fault in Our Stars by himself in the theater so he'd be able to talk to his daughter about it when she got back from the summer with her mom."

"Now, that's a good dad."

"Yep." Sara pulls her cuffs down over her fingertips. "I talked to Tim last night. He'd just got back from dinner with some friends. He kept talking about this woman he met."

"This woman?" My eyebrow cocks, through no will of my own. "Are you concerned?"

"What? No. Tim would never."

I nod. Tim's a great guy, but he's still a guy. Once, early in my marriage, Sara suggested I give Karl 100% of my trust until he gave me a reason to doubt him. It was cute.

"What did he say about her?"

She frowns at me. "Nothing, really. He said he thought I'd like her."

"Mm-hm."

She rolls her eyes. Sara doesn't get jealous. Or she does, but she doesn't admit it. All these years, I still can't tell.

Lucy's talking to a little boy who sits on the swing next to her. I can't hear what's being said, but after a few moments, he gets up to push her. She remembers to pump her legs like I told her: knees bent as she swings back; legs straight as she sails forward.

"They're practicing drills at school in case there's another shooting," I say. I think of the week before when Lucy came home to tell me and I just nodded along, not trusting myself to speak. They'd sent no letters home to warn parents this would happen.

"Does she understand what it's for?"

"They told the kids that it had something to do with a moose, I think."

"A moose?"

I shrug. "Lucy said one time there was a moose in the playground and everyone had to stay inside. Lockdown."

Sara shakes her head.

"They taught them to hide in a closet and be very quiet. And if someone knocks on the door, they still have to be very quiet. She explained it all like it was a game and I didn't know what to say."

"Being a kid was so much simpler for us," Sara says and I agree. "All we had were fire drills."

I thought things had always been simple for us, but at some point they stopped being simple for Sara and she just never told me. It wasn't until the summer after her college graduation that she explained to me why she had to give up driving.

We were in the parking lot of a Walmart and for some reason I remember it as if she was sitting in the driver's seat, but obviously that's impossible. Sara never owned a car. She borrowed her parents' Taurus in the summers and I drove whenever we went out together. I'd always thought it was because she went to college in New York City, but it turned out to be a bit more complicated.

When she told me, she was shaking and avoiding eye contact. It had been a secret for so long. Years. I didn't really understand when she said the word *progressive*. I just thought it explained why she was such a klutz.

Lucy runs over to us and wants to know if we've been watching.

"You swung so high!" Sara says and Lucy beams.

"What's your friend's name?" I ask.

"Oh, I don't think he had one." Lucy says.

Sara bursts out laughing, but I'm mortified. "Lucy, everybody has a name!" I tell her to hurry back and ask him. "And this time, offer to push *him* on the swing."

Lucy sighs heavily and heads back to the swing set. Sara's still laughing.

"You can't just laugh at her," I scold and she tries to stop.

"I'm sorry," she says, but I know she doesn't really get it. How could she? She's not responsible for the psychological development of a human being.

If Lucy thinks it's funny to imagine other people don't have their own identities, she might turn out totally self-centered, thinking the world is full of extras in the movie of her life. She could grow up to be a tyrant or a sociopath or a doormat, and it will be my fault. I will have been too strict or not strict enough. I will damage her self-esteem so that she never feels good enough or I will tell her she's beautiful so much that she'll think it's all she has to offer. I'll give her unconditional praise and she'll become a slacker or I'll be withholding and she'll never learn to trust people.

No matter what I do, she'll end up talking about me to her therapist someday, making a list of the ways I failed her.

"There, see, she's pushing him now," Sara says, pointing.

Over Sara's shoulder, I can see a blond woman sitting in a turquoise Honda in the parking lot. She seems to be crying.

And the world keeps turning.

Before we leave, Lucy asks if she can push Sara's chair to the car. When she was three, she liked to surprise everyone by pushing the chair without warning. Sara was a good sport about it, but it was always so embarrassing. We'd taught her to ask permission. I kneel at the edge of the sandbox and pry a plastic shovel out of Grace's hands. I'm ready for the tears, but to my surprise, she gives it up relatively easily. She never seems to get mad the way Lucy does, giving me hope that her toddler years might not kill me.

After the girls are in bed, I stand at the kitchen sink and scrub the pans from dinner. Karl steps behind me and wraps his arms around my waist.

"You can do that tomorrow," he says like he's offering a gift. He's not offering to do the dishes for me. He's giving me permission to do it another day. And as he bends to kiss my neck, I understand why. He'd like to have sex.

I wriggle away from him and turn on the faucet. I already have plenty on my plate for tomorrow. And I don't want Grammy waking up to a sink full of dishes in the morning.

"Go find the cat," I tell him. Muffin was gone all day (likely in order to avoid the attention of the girls) and Grammy seemed distraught as she tried to call him in after dinner. I convinced her to go to bed, promising I'd make sure he came in before going to bed myself.

Karl grumbles and goes outside while putting on his jacket. He's reaching for his cigarettes before the door slaps shut behind him.

It's not that I don't enjoy sex with my husband. I do. I remember it fondly. But by the end of the day, I'm generally too tired to do much more than that. He kisses my neck when I'm up to my elbows in dirty dishes and I just want to laugh. I mean, it's a lovely idea, but I have about six hours before the girls will be awake again. Let's get real.

A few months ago, I'd encouraged him to send me naughty texts during the day so we could save time on foreplay when he got home from work. They started sweet and sexy and we traded messages back and forth as his responses kept getting dirtier. Finally, I'd called him. "Karl! How can you talk like that to me? I am the mother of your children!"

There had been no sex that night.

Out the window, I watch the burning ember of his cigarette in the darkness. He claps his hands and calls out. I set the last glass in the dish drainer and open the back door.

"You don't clap for cats, dummy." I step outside and hug myself in the cold.

"We never had cats," he says like that explains it. I never had cats either. Some things you just know.

"Getting cold," I say and my words become smoke in the darkness.

He stomps out his cigarette as I show him how to make kissy noises and he wraps his warm arms around me. "Like this?" he says with his lips against mine.

I giggle and squirm as the cat emerges from the shadows.

"Oh, see. It worked," he says and Muffin twines himself in an infinity symbol around our ankles, purring, as Karl holds me tight.

Delilah: Friday

I get up so early, I can't identify the paint color on the wall and I haven't been here long enough to remember what it is. I sit in the dark silence of the unfamiliar kitchen hugging a mug full of coffee, thinking: *what am I doing here?* and: *really, what am I doing?* as the room brightens in increments and I start to hear water in the pipes and footsteps and other evidence that suggests I am not alone in the house after all.

The walls are a pretty sage and I wonder who chose the color.

Sadie gets up first, her hair still wet from the shower, her make up not yet obscuring one set of features and inventing another. She stretches and yawns over her orange juice and granola, sitting with her bare feet tucked under her thighs. She talks with her mouth full.

"How did you decide you wanted to be a social worker?"

For some reason, I find myself debating over whether to make up a more impressive story. "I watched a lot of Oprah in high school," I say. "I thought I'd be a psychiatrist and heal the world."

"The world?" Sadie has bright blue polish on her toenails. She's laughing at me, but it isn't mean.

"Oh, yes. I had very grandiose ideas." I'm laughing at me, too.

"What changed?"

"When you get to college, you get to study things you've never been exposed to before. In high school, there are like ten subjects and half of them are different kinds of math you'll never use. But in college, there's anthropology and philosophy and 19th century romantic literature and silent film and political theory and graphic art. You might go in thinking you want to be a doctor, but you don't even know all the possibilities yet."

"Hm." She looks away and I wonder if I shouldn't have said *doctor*, should have kept it more hypothetical. She finishes her juice in silence and then looks back at me, holding the empty glass to her chest. "What do you think about the Peace Corps?"

I don't really know anything about the Peace Corps, besides the fact that it does still exist. I have a vague impression of them as hippy do-gooders in the seventies, returning from a year in Africa to protest the war in Vietnam. I remember a friend in college who had done Teach for America, but the kids I worked with weren't candidates for these kinds of community service programs. If they wanted to see the world, or even just escape their home towns, the military was the only option for them. I often wonder what would happen if politicians actually followed through on their promises to make college free. Who would fight in their wars?

"You can do amazing things in the Peace Corps." This seems vague, but probably true.

"I was thinking about what you were saying the other night at dinner. About traveling. I don't think I need to go backpacking across Europe or something like that. It feels too . . ." Sadie squints as if the perfect word is out in the yard, beyond the glass doors. "Aimless." She nods in apparent agreement with herself and looks me in the eye. "But it could be good for me to experience life in another country, right?"

"Oh my god, Sadie, I think it would be fantastic."

"I could really be of use somewhere. Give back. Get out of my comfort zone."

I'm nodding along. "I think it would be such a great opportunity. You'd learn the kinds of things you'd never learn here. Do you have any idea where they might send you?"

"I was looking at their site last night. They have programs in the Philippines, South Africa, Panama." She's talking fast and grinning more with every word. "Fiji, Cambodia. Some places I've never heard of. Everywhere."

"You should have an adventure before you get to all the boring work of adulthood."

"But this would be work, too. It'd be both."

I reach out to pat her upper arm. "Yes, best of both worlds."

"I wish I thought my dad would see it that way. Something tells me he won't be such a fan of the Peace Corps."

"The Peace Corps?" David's voice is so deep and sharp, I pull my hand away from Sadie as if we've been caught plotting a school prank.

He storms into the kitchen and slaps the table in front of me. "Who do you think you are?" he shouts. "Putting these ideas in her head? Getting her to throw away everything we've worked toward?"

I blink. David's never yelled at me before this moment. We weren't the kind of siblings who'd grown up testing each other's boundaries. When he'd come home from college or visited for the holidays, he always felt like an honored guest. We cleaned the house for his arrival; we were on our best behavior, making polite conversation, avoiding awkward silences. If I'd ever broken something he treasured, he'd have been too polite to get mad. We were careful with each other.

Before I can answer, Sadie jumps to her feet. "Don't talk about me like I'm not even in the room!"

David's head swings toward her and his eyebrows knit together in something resembling confusion.

"And it's not Delilah's fault anyway," she continues, crossing her arms. "It was my idea." She throws her shoulders back, defiantly, and I feel like she's defending me against an armored tank. The kitchen has become Tiananmen Square.

"We were just talking," I say quietly, hoping to calm things down.

Sadie looks at the clock, realizes she has to finish getting ready for school, and leaves the room in a huff, depositing her dishes in the sink with a crash before she goes. David shakes his head at me and starts making coffee, breathing loudly as if it has suddenly become a process that requires his complete attention. I wait for him to apologize. I give him five whole minutes, counted out on that same stove clock that prompted Sadie's exit, but he has nothing to say.

I carry my mug to the sink and feel disappointed when it lands soundlessly. I stomp barefoot to the guest room and pull the door shut behind me as hard as I can, but it just rubs a gentle friction against the plush carpeting and sounds like a dry cough.

Once Sadie and David have left for the day, I go back to sleep. In my dreams, I replay the scene from breakfast only now David's red face morphs into my father's, who never actually yelled at me before either. There was never any *wait until your father gets home* threatening when I was growing up. My mother was the disciplinarian; my father was a pushover.

I don't know how long David had been standing in the doorway, listening to Sadie and me talk, but he's overreacting, wound so tight, Sadie's slightest exhalation sends him into a spin. A little distance will be good for both of them, wherever she decides to go after graduation. It could be really good for her, a year of service, a year to think about what to do with her life. It is her life. Perhaps David's too close to see that.

When I wake, it's past noon; I'm sweaty and disoriented. I'll be on my own for dinner tonight. Sadie's staying at a friend's house and David has "plans." The way he said the word, avoiding eye contact, made me wonder if it was a date.

Now, there's someone who needs to get laid.

The bookshelf in the living room holds mostly science books and nonfiction, so I slip into Sadie's room in the hope that she has a better selection. I'm not disappointed. She has a bookshelf full of fiction organized in such a way that I feel like I can chart her evolving taste over a lifetime. The bottom shelf has a series of Choose-Your-Own-Adventure books, *The Lion, the Witch and the Wardrobe, Alice in Wonderland, The Secret Garden*. The second shelf is chock full of YA: John Green, Jodi Picoult. There's a section of classics: *Catcher and the Rye, Pride and Prejudice, Brave New World*. I'm actually impressed by a few on the top shelf: *The Corrections, A Visit from the Goon Squad, The Goldfinch*. I haven't even read that last one. At the end of the top row, I see a familiar brown cover. I slide it out and hold the weight of it in my hand. The spine is barely creased and I wonder if it's ever been read.

Barbara Kingsolver is from Tucson; that's part of why I'd chosen it for her. The other part was something deeper. I'd read it years ago and had always wanted to pass it along.

I sit on the edge of Sadie's bed, the blankets in a tangled mess. With my fingertips, I trace the impression her head has left in the pillow.

I pull my cell phone from the back pocket of my jeans and call Leslie.

"Dee!" That's what she calls me because I was still introducing myself that way when I met her, years after graduating college. Eventually, I decided Lilah sounded more professional, and I'd used that for a while, but I'd stopped after my mother died. It hurt too much to hear someone call me that when it wasn't her.

"How are you?" she asks and she manages to sound like she genuinely wants to know the answer. It isn't just a platitude. The way she asks makes me stop to consider the matter.

"I'm okay."

"Really?" It seems I can't convince her either.

I lie sideways across Sadie's bed and stare at the ceiling. "It's been good connecting with my niece, even if David doesn't think so."

"What does that mean?"

I start to talk about Sadie, how smart she is, how beautiful. And maybe just a little bit lost. "She's basically grown up without a mother," I say. It isn't totally true, I suppose, though I can't imagine a mother only checking in a few months a year. How much you'd miss from one summer to the next. If I had a kid, I wouldn't let her grow up without me. "I think she likes having a woman to talk to. David wants her to go to college next year, but she's started talking about taking a year off and he thinks it's my fault."

"Is it?"

I laugh, pretending to be offended. "I've just been hearing her out."

"Mm-hm. Well, don't wear out your welcome," she says and then she thinks better of it. "Or do wear it out. When are you coming home?"

"I guess I'm not in any rush. What is there to come home for?"

She doesn't answer and in the silence, I press my palm against the cover of the book in my lap. I decide to ask Sadie if she read it. I'll ask casually, like it doesn't matter.

"Do you ever think about having kids?" I wonder into the phone.

"Kids?" Leslie says it like a dirty word, like she's looked behind the refrigerator and found them crawling around in their own filth, like they're maggots. "Not really. I've always felt I give what I have to the kids I work with. There's not much left after that. I always thought you felt the same."

That is how I've felt. I remember saying as much when we've talked about it in the past. "Do you think I'd make a good mom?"

"Where is this coming from?"

I sigh. "Lately, I'm looking at my life and wondering what I have to show for it."

"Well, a kid won't fix that."

"No?"

"No." She sounds so sure I want to ask her what will fix it, but I don't want to sound pathetic.

"I think the world needs people who aren't devoting all their life's energy to their specific offspring," she says.

I think she has a point. If I was a mother, I wouldn't be able to do anything else. I'd be consumed by it. Maybe knowing that is what's made me put it off. Not that I've ever been in the kind of relationship where the question would be asked in the first place. I'd wasted years with Marty, important child-bearing years, letting my eggs dry up while we fell apart slowly. I had to have known he was never going to give me a family. Of course, I'd known.

I change the subject. She gives me the latest installment of workplace gossip, tells me about her mother's upcoming hip replacement. Before we hang up, she reminds me there's still time to have a kid if I want. She says she misses me. She feels so close, but as soon as I press the hang up button, she's gone and I'm alone again.

I'm wearing a T-shirt and underpants, burrowed deep in the bed covers. I scroll through the photos on my laptop. He's in so few of them. They're all castles carved out of mountains or ruins or pyramids. But here he stands with an arm around a local. I read the caption over and over but it's still just Bakari, who'd graciously shown him around that day. It doesn't tell me what I want to know.

Which is what?

I reach for my glass of wine on the night stand. I'd gotten out of the habit of drinking alcohol of any kind while I was with Marty. I never kept it in my apartment because I didn't want it to be a trigger. I never drank when we went out together because that meant he wouldn't drink and I never drank when we went out separately because I knew I'd need to pick him up at some point.

The wine warms my belly. It softens the sharp edges of the room and the sharper edges of my memory.

Tim's business card has become worn between my fingers.

He answers on the second ring and I tell him it's Delilah, because that's the name he'll recognize. I apologize for calling so late.

"Oh, it's not that late," he says and I think I hear him stifle a yawn. "What can I do for you?"

"I was thinking about what we were talking about at dinner the other night."

"Oh?"

I pull the cord on the lamp, plunging the room into darkness. I press the phone against my ear until it hurts; it's just the two of us.

"I need to start doing some of those things I always planned to do. What you said about your trip really inspired me."

"Well, thanks. What were you planning?"

"For starters, I want to learn to ride a motorcycle. David said he took your class a few years back." This is hard for me to imagine, but he swore he got a perfect score on the test.

"That's how we met," Tim says.

"So how would I sign up for your class? Is there time to get in this weekend?"

"As in tomorrow?"

"Yeah. Would that be a problem?"

"I think we're already full up for tomorrow, but listen—" He pauses here and I hold my breath, awaiting a confession. "You don't need to take the class."

"I don't?"

"No, I could just give you a lesson in a parking lot some afternoon off the books."

"Really?" It sounds illicit.

"Sure."

I think of his girlfriend, wonder what she's like. Will she be jealous of him giving me private lessons? Do they ride motorcycles together? I imagine her taking off her helmet and shaking her hair loose in slow motion. Does she listen while he tells her what it's like to be motherless? Does she understand?

"It's not for everyone," he's saying. "It might be good to get a feel for whether it's something you want to pursue when you go back home."

"I haven't decided," I say and I know he thinks I'm talking about the motorcycle, but I'm not. I could get a place here. I don't have to stay indefinitely in my brother's guest room and I don't have to go back east where the water will soon be frozen silent.

I thank Tim for the offer and say I'm looking forward to it. When he reminds me that we'll see each other at dinner next week, I pretend I need to be reminded. He hangs up first.

Yesterday, I drove downtown and passed a dozen apartment

complexes advertising special deals. "One month free rent!" the signs shouted. I walked the sidewalks of Fourth Avenue, a block or so away from the center of campus, full of quaint, eclectic shops. A pizza place with outdoor seating, a thrift store with mannequins wearing purple wigs, several tattoo parlors, a feminist book shop, a bar with pool tables. I imagined Sadie spending her afternoons this way a year from now, seeming like any other bored hipster trying so hard to look like she wasn't trying to look a certain way.

Everyone was younger than me, except for the homeless people; maybe it was the fact that it was mid-afternoon on a weekday. There was a help-wanted sign in the window of the vegan tea house and I pictured myself here, riding my bike home to one of the bungalows down a side street. Or maybe I'd travel on the street car.

I could be Delilah here, whoever that is.

David: Friday

On the drive to school, I can't tell if Sadie isn't speaking to me or I'm not speaking to her. All I know is it sure is quiet. A little NPR might distract from the fury coming off of her in nearly visible thunderbolts as she glares out the passenger side window, but neither of us move to switch the radio on. Her body is pressed close to the door, the farthest away from me that she can get.

I can still hear her shrill voice at breakfast, so offended. "Don't talk about me like I'm not even in the room!" she said and I still don't understand. How else could I say something to Delilah without referring to Sadie in the third person. That doesn't mean I was ignoring her presence. I'm stuck on this, though, of course, it's not the point of the argument.

But, as with most arguments, it's about one thing for her and something totally different for me.

It reminds me of fights with her mother. I approached them logically: A led to B, which led to C. But confidence would desert me as I realized she was using a different alphabet or a 3D model of lighted points in a constellation and my argument would skitter across the expanding space between us, upended by gravity, my carefully ordered note cards littering the floor at my feet.

By the time Sadie was old enough to understand what we were saying, there was no need to spell out angry words. We'd given up arguing. We'd given up trying to change each other. At first, I thought it might be a good thing, a natural shift in a maturing relationship.

But now I think we'd given up on something more, something fundamental. We'd given up on the idea of being understood. And isn't that really what marriage is, if you're lucky? If you get it right? You've decided to spend your life with someone who has promised, at the most basic level, to see you. Every day. To be a living record of your existence.

That's what separates single people from married ones. Being seen.

At a red light, Sadie suddenly turns to me and crosses her arms. I don't look at her, but I can feel the scowl, the heat of her piercing stare. It's quiet enough in the car that I hear her uneven intake of breath. "I'm going to be eighteen, you know." Her voice is shaking and I wonder how much of it is anger, how much fear.

The light changes and I drive through the intersection without a word. I let her consider I may not answer. Then I pull into a grocery store parking lot, slide into a spot beside a cranberry minivan, and release my seatbelt. It makes a satisfying crack as I turn to face her. I'm startled to see tears in her eyes and I bite back the frustration in my voice.

"I know that," I say softly. I touch her knee and she looks away, her jaw set. She is so beautiful. Yes, she will be eighteen. And twenty-one and twenty-five and thirty-three. She will break somebody's heart. She will be somebody's mother. She has no idea how fast it all goes; she's just in a hurry to get it started.

I wiggle her knee until she looks at me again. I nod. "Tell me."

She takes another jagged breath. "I don't have to go to college next year."

I take this in. Just breathing. My anger is not at her. Before Delilah arrived, Sadie was laser-focused on the future. She's taking an advanced anatomy class at the local community college. She has a calendar on the wall of her bedroom where she marks all the relevant deadlines: application due dates, career fairs, yearbook submissions. Just last week, I overheard her telling Sara she planned to test out of certain required freshman courses. One week with my alluring, carefree little sister, and all of that goes out the window? "Delilah went to college, you know. She has a degree."

She tosses her dark curls. "A lot of good it's done her."

"Uh? I'd say so."

"Dad, she's unemployed."

"Right now." And what does that even mean to someone like Delilah, with no one depending on her, no responsibilities?

"She can't even get a job in her field."

"Did she tell you that?"

Sadie shrugs, superior, in the know. "Haven't you talked to her? She's been here a week."

This barb has its intended affect: I'm shamed. Delilah has cooked dinner all week; it's been fantastic. When I get home from work, there's been some pleasant dinnertime chit-chat followed by an hour or so of television before we all retire to our respective corners of the house.

Except Wednesday night when Delilah and Tim had argued the uselessness of a college degree. I saw Sadie sit back in her chair, her eyelids drooping to half-mast as her mind worked. What had Delilah been thinking?

"I'm afraid you're getting swept up in Delilah's romantic ideas." I'm afraid she's getting caught up in Delilah's mid-life crisis, is more like it.

Sadie throws up her hands and looks to the ceiling. "As if I don't have a mind of my own?"

"You never talked about joining the Peace Corps before she got here."

She can't argue with that. Instead, she lets out a dramatic sigh. "I'm not talking about not going to college at all. I'd just be delaying it a year."

That's something, I guess, but it's the loss of momentum that concerns me. How many kids take that year off and then it becomes two years? Twenty? "Becoming a doctor takes a long time. Can you afford to take a year off to go gallivanting around the world?"

"Gallivanting?" she scoffs. "Imagine all the things I'd learn that I'd never get the chance to learn here. It could be great experience."

That doesn't sound totally unreasonable, but I'm far from giving in. "Have you talked to your guidance counselor about this?"

"Not yet."

I sigh. We sit together wordlessly as I stare out the windshield, gripping the steering wheel. "Well, maybe we should start there?"

She nods enthusiastically. "Okay."

She's already going to be late to first period so I decide we might as well stop at a drive-thru for coffee. I switch on the radio and let her pick the station.

I always dreamed of having my own office with a window and a secretary on the other side of the door who would speak to me through an intercom. She would take my coat when she greeted me in the morning and know how I liked my coffee. I don't know where I got this idea. Television? My own father didn't have a job like this. Even once he'd sobered up on account of Delilah, his jobs were strictly blue-collar and always changing.

What I have is slightly different from the fantasy: no window, a secretary I share with four of my colleagues. I hang my own coat and get my own coffee. But I have something precious: job security. I've worked at the same company for twenty years; it seems I belong to the last generation that aspires to that.

I sit behind my desk and reach for Sadie's most recent school picture. The photos from previous years are squeezed in behind it in the frame; I never know what to do with the older ones. I can't just throw them away. I pull apart the glass and spread them all across the surface of the desk in front of me.

When Sadie was little, even before Janet left, I'd been the one to comb through her dark curls in the morning, spritz them with de-tangler, deal with the tears. Pigtails were my favorite, even if getting the center part straight was a nightmare. In third grade, Sadie had to tell me pigtails had fallen out of favor. It was all ponytails or barrettes; pigtails were for babies. That loss had been one of the small heartbreaks in a series of heartbreaks over the course of her mad dash to grow up.

I had been determined to give Sadie the easy childhood I never had. The divorce felt like an admission of my failure to do that. I felt less a failure as a husband, since Janet was at least as much to blame for that as I was. But Sadie was an innocent; she hadn't chosen me as a father any more than I'd chosen mine. Being able to stay married may not be the only measure of a good parent, but surely it is one.

Before I leave for the day, I brush my teeth in the restroom at work and go over my date's stats: Maryanne, realtor, fifty-three, Episcopalian, blond hair, brown eyes, 5'6". In her profile, she called her figure average, but when we met, I thought she was being overly modest. On our first date, we swapped war stories. She's been divorced for six years, has two sons who are both in college now and an ex-husband who lives in town. They have not remained friends, which always makes more sense to me than the opposite. I don't understand amicable divorces. If you could find a way to be friends, why would you break up your family? How could you inflict that sort of damage on your children unless you were sure staying together would be worse?

After that dinner, I walked Maryanne to her car and kissed her goodnight. She hadn't really kissed me back and I assumed I'd blown it. I drove home kicking myself for the miscalculation. But, how were you to know? Some women wanted to be kissed on the first date and others thought it was incredibly insulting. And you couldn't just ask because that showed a lack of confidence or it put the woman on the defensive. If you kissed a woman who didn't want to be kissed, it was a blow to your ego. But if you didn't kiss her when she wanted to be kissed, you hurt her feelings.

It was exhausting.

Anyway, it turned out I hadn't blown it after all because she texted me on Monday and we got together for coffee. I don't know if that counts as a second date, but I think it should because even though it was brief, when I walked her back to her car, she pounced on me and we made out against her SUV like I can't remember doing since my twenties. I'd had to straighten my hair in the rearview mirror before going back to work.

Tonight, I get to the restaurant after she's already arrived and worry about the message that sends. I glance at my watch as I sit across from her, reassuring myself that I'm not late. I say hello, suddenly concerned that I should have kissed her before I sat down. She tells me I look nice and I cringe, unable to accept the compliment since I know I should have complimented her first. She does look nice; she's wearing a deep green blouse with the top two buttons undone and revealing just the slightest hint of cleavage.

"I'm so bad at this," I say.

"At what?"

I gesture back and forth between us. "This. It's changed so much since twenty-five years ago and I wasn't particularly good at it back then."

She smiles, setting me at ease. She's wearing more makeup than she had on our previous dates. Makeup is so odd, especially eye shadow. At least the other kinds of makeup seem to be designed to emphasize what is naturally there: make the cheeks rosier, draw attention to the lips, outline the eyes and extend existing lashes. I can imagine scientific explanations for these things that are based on evolution, on making the woman appear healthier, more fertile. But how do colored eyelids contribute to that impression? Green or purple or gray eyelids?

Maryanne's eyelids are silver; they sparkle as she bats her thick lashes at me and reaches for my hand. "I think you're doing just fine," she says and I feel that flutter in my chest.

We order wine with the meal. She talks about her youngest son who's in his first year at UNM. He calls home so often she's starting to worry about him. I talk about the argument I had with my sister that morning and Maryanne echoes my belief:

"People without kids just don't understand." She twists strands of linguini on her fork. "That last year of high school is so precarious. I've done it twice. I didn't breathe that sigh of relief until sometime after the first week of classes."

"What about that empty nest we're warned about?"

She shakes her head, chewing. I wait for her reply. "I'm here to tell you something about the empty nest." She points her fork at me. "It's fantastic. I mean, I know it's still early, but I've been enjoying my quiet weekends, reading a book with a cup of tea."

"So wild."

She shrugs. "Sometimes it really does feel wild, though. After twenty years of their activities and television shows and food preferences, I'm getting to know what *I* like to do, to watch, to eat. I'm getting to know me again."

I lift my wine glass. "Let's drink to that. To getting to know you."

This time, when I walk her to her car, she asks if I'd like to follow her back to her place for "a nightcap." My heart races and I nod my head. We kiss some more and then we get into our separate cars.

When you're a single parent, sex never just happens. You have to get babysitters and plan ahead and skirt out in the early morning before accidentally traumatizing someone's child. But Maryanne's house is newly empty. The idea gives me the kind of thrill I once got when someone told me their parents were away.

I park on her street and watch as the garage door grumbles to a close behind her. It's a two car garage attached to a large ranch-style home. This must be the house she got in the divorce, big enough for a once growing family. I wonder, despite her brave face at dinner, if she feels lonely in a house this big now that she's on her own. I wonder if I will.

I see a series of lights switch on inside and I walk to the front door, which opens before I can knock. Maryanne takes my hand and leads me down the hall. In the bedroom, she steps close and pushes my jacket from my shoulders as she kisses me. She lays it carefully in a corner chair and turns, holding her elbows, suddenly shy.

"Do you need anything? A drink?"

I shake my head and reach for her, holding her at the waist and pulling her toward me. Her silk blouse feels amazing under my hands and I slide them up and down her back several times before I begin to undo the buttons. Slowly. When I reach the last one, I step away. The lights are low but she doesn't move to turn them off completely. She shrugs the silk from her shoulders and it pools at her feet. For a moment, she lets me look at her in her black lace bra and skirt.

"Lovely," I murmur; the ability to form complete sentences has deserted me.

She smiles wickedly then and starts on the buttons of my shirt. She's much faster than I was. She nudges me backward and as I sit at the foot of the bed, she kneels in front of me and kisses her way down my stomach. When I suck in my gut, she giggles.

She undoes my belt buckle as she kisses my neck and presses her body against me. I find the clasp of her bra. It has been so long since I did this, but it's all coming back to me.

She pulls away and I search her face. "Are we going too fast? We can stop."

She reaches out and strokes the side of my face. "Do you want to stop?" That wicked smile again.

I glance down at the part of me that lacks any gentlemanly impulse to play it cool. Maryanne touches me through my boxers and winks. Then she slows things down by removing my shoes and laying the rest of my clothing on the chair with my jacket. She sets my cell phone on the night stand and I feel no need to explain why I have to keep it near.

When she pulls a foil wrapped condom out of the top drawer, I realize that what's about to happen is not the result of a whim. This comes as a relief, and for some reason, I think it's even sexier.

She stands in front of me and lifts my hands to her hips, helping my fingers find the tiny zipper. The skirt falls to her ankles and I press my face against her, breathing her scent as I squeeze her buttocks. She lets out a little gasp.

Once we're under the sheets, she lets me take off her bra and I understand this is how it will be. I'm aware of imagining a future when I might grow to take all of this for granted as routine. But for now, the feel of her bare breasts against my naked chest is electric. She wraps her legs around my waist and whispers in my ear as I concentrate on reciting the periodic table in my mind. When she comes, I feel her shudder. I'm thinking: AU, gold. I brush her hair across her forehead, kiss her deeply and finish a close, grateful second.

We lie together, sweaty and quiet at first.

"Close your eyes," she says and I obey. I feel her rise from the bed. When she returns, she passes me a tiny paper cup of water. We talk then, about everything and nothing, our first heart breaks, our favorite television shows. I lie on my back; she leans on one elbow, the fingers of her other hand tracing circles on my chest. It gets very late.

"Can you stay?" she asks.

It would be easy to make an excuse, but Sadie is sleeping at a friend's house. I think of Delilah. Will she wait up? Will she even notice if I don't come home? I decide I don't care. And I don't want to make excuses. "I'd love that."

Maryanne presses against me, her curves softening my edges.

Sara: Saturday

We're running late. Grace vomited on Ally's dress just as she was heading out the door to pick me up and she had to change. I still think she looks beautiful, but the other dress was purchased specifically for this event and she won't stop talking about it. It was ice blue, apparently, with an asymmetrical neckline and glass beading on the bodice. The one she's wearing now is a deep purple satin that displays a tasteful, enviable bit of cleavage.

"It brings out the violet in your eyes," I tell her. "You look like a young Elizabeth Taylor."

"How young?"

I look her up and down, pretending think it over. "Thirty-two."

"I'll take it."

I hate dresses. I wear a black suit and floral silk blouse, confident that Ethan is not a stickler for wedding dress codes. I feel more comfortable about my outfit when I see Ethan's "best man" in a powder blue tuxedo and Mohawk. If gender is on a spectrum, this person would likely place a rainbow flag right at the point in the center.

Ethan's mother lives in California and doesn't fly; I've never met her and don't get the sense that they're close. Colin's parents make up for her absence by being big and boisterous, laughing and crying in the front row. No one walks down the aisle; both grooms are poised at the front of the church in complementary gray suits and when the officiant asks who presents them to be wed, Colin's parents call out with enthusiasm: "We do!"

The ceremony is so short, it makes our struggle to find parking seem like a wasted effort. That's how it is with weddings. People plan them a year in advance, getting invested in details they won't even have time to notice.

A decade ago, Ally threatened to cancel her own wedding over round tables. We'd been up until four in the morning, tying ribbons on programs for the ceremony. It took two hours to get our hair done and when we got back to the house, Ally found out they'd delivered the wrong tables to the reception. Circles instead of squares.

Ally squeezed the finishing touches onto the wedding cake she'd designed, sniffling, red splotches ruining her bridal complexion. She pointed her chin upward, tears jumping from her lashes. "There isn't going to be a wedding," she announced, even as she held the tube of white frosting. The bridesmaids were starting to arrive by then and each took a turn reasoning with her. Her mother pulled at her hair; her father paced in the yard.

I managed to coax her into the wedding gown even though I understood that there wouldn't be a wedding. *Yes, yes, but let's just see how it looks.*

Once the dress was on, Ally took one look in the mirror and forgot all about the tables.

At Ally's wedding, I couldn't wear pants – I was the maid of honor. I did, however, wear tennis shoes painted celedon to match my dress. I held the best man's arm in a death grip as I wobbled my sleep-deprived self up the aisle, passing lit candles on the end of every pew and considering how quickly the tiny, ancient church could burn to the ground.

Ally appeared at the church door on her father's arm, her dark hair falling in soft waves down her back, her hourglass figure wrapped in white satin. She looked so beautiful, I cried.

Ethan's reception is at an orchard a short drive from the church.

"Look, Ally, round tables," I say as we find our seats. She sticks her tongue out at me.

There are a dozen of these tables inside a rustic old barn. The centerpieces are candles in mason jars covered with fall leaves in various shades of red and orange. I wonder who was up last night making them. There are eight other people at our table, all of them women.

I recognize the woman on Ally's right. She's cut her blond ringlets close to her scalp, making the curl even tighter. "You remember Juliet," I say to Ally, in case she doesn't. They met once long ago, in another lifetime. "Ethan and Juliet were friends since high school, just like us."

Ally and Juliet shake hands. "Does he introduce you as his *oldest* friend?" Ally asks.

Juliet laughs and stands up to hug me. We've only met twice in real life, but in the time between, I've seen so much of her on

Ethan's Facebook page, it feels like I know her well.

She's wearing a flowy pink maxi dress, a hot pink Gerbera daisy fastened to her hair with bobby pins. She's tall and her strappy silver heels make her taller. She has bare arms and I wonder how she isn't freezing.

The last time I saw her was two summers ago. Her son was just learning to walk. Every few steps, he'd fall against the cushion of his diaper and look up at her, wide eyed. "You're okay!" she'd shout to him and he'd smile, relieved, and get back up.

"How old is Jamal now?" I ask.

"He's three," she says, reaching for her phone to show us the evidence.

"My oldest just turned five," Ally says and they get lost in a conversation about their children. I nod along, scrolling through images of a boy with tan skin and bright blue eyes.

It's not that I dislike children – I just find most of them boring. I love Ally's girls to pieces; every word they utter is either hilarious or brilliant. But other people's children are a generic blur of inconsequential cuteness. Their daily dilemmas and insights do not intrigue me. I hand the phone back and I've already forgotten the boy's face.

In the past week, I've learned to spot the baby-haters whenever we go out. Sleeping in the carriage, Grace was eyed suspiciously by patrons at the coffee shop. They'd shoot nasty looks at the slightest babble. As she sat at the front of the grocery cart, she waved at strangers and squealed with joy. I don't understand why anyone would be mad about that. I'm sort of envious. Imagine being so full of joy, you just have to shriek.

The first time I met Juliet was a decade ago when Ethan was living in Boston for a brief speck of time before he moved to England. I'd just graduated from college, Ally and Karl were planning their wedding, Tucson hadn't yet occurred to me. Ethan had a going away party at an Indian place in the city. Ally and I took the train in and for several stops, I clung to a metal pole and concentrated on the placement of my feet, praying for a seat to open up.

Juliet's hair was longer then, tied back in a scarf. She was quieter too; I remember thinking she was shy. Now she strikes me as bubbly and animated. Maybe that's just part of growing up, learning how to feel comfortable in your own skin.

I don't remember the food or the conversation at Ethan's party. What I do remember is that at the end of the night, I slipped in an icy parking lot and fell in front of everyone. I ripped my pants and bloodied a knee, but what really hurt was the *in front of everyone* part. Ally helped me up and made a joke about cocktails, knowing I'd had none. She held my arm tighter as we walked back to the T station.

Between slipping on ice or shivering until I fell down, winter shrunk my world more that year than any other.

Ally and I had always planned to get a place together after I graduated, but by the time I got home from college, she was already living with Karl. Meanwhile, my life seemed to be having the opposite trajectory. I got dumped that December, right before Christmas, and spent that winter alone in a lousy one-bedroom apartment, eating Cup-o-Noodles in my pajamas and working on spreadsheets for my dad's business. I was convinced Ally only remembered I existed when she needed me to help with *wedding shit*, as I called it in my head. In January, when Ethan followed some guy across an ocean, I felt well and truly deserted.

I'd spent several years after my diagnosis without noticeable symptoms. Telling no one meant I never had to think about it. My abilities changed incrementally year by year so that I never thought to be grateful I could walk up stairs without a railing until I couldn't do it anymore.

Someday, maybe as soon as six months in the future, I knew I'd look back on that winter and remember all the things that had been so much easier, things I had taken for granted at the time. Meanwhile, my mind would last and last long after my body was gone. I was twenty-three and miserable, already past my physical peak. Trapped inside while the snow piled up into March, I came to the realization that things would never be even this good again.

Waiters bring us food on ivory plates. I got the chicken; Ally got the fish. We go around the table, introducing ourselves. Three of them are fellow painter friends of Ethan, one is a gallery owner, and the last three are Colin's much younger cousins. I'm relieved that the table is too big to support prolonged group conversations, and we form several cliques. Juliet and Ally and I are one.

"How's your trip so far?" Juliet asks me.

"Oh, it's been great. Cramming a lot in. A week's never long enough." This is mostly true, though I already miss my Tucson life with my boyfriend and my cat and my very own bed. Christine and Becca drove up from New York and stayed over at my hotel for a night. My aunt and I visited my grandmother in the retirement home yesterday. She was sharp and chatty, full of gossip about her neighbors. "Most days, I've been with Ally and her girls at the park, the hotel pool, or the mall. Geez, have you been to the mall lately?"

"I hate the mall, but Jamal loves it."

"I bet he does."

The mall is a very different place from what I remember as a child. Now it's an amusement park. There are coin operated motorbikes, carousels, and photo booths. Between stores, projectors on the ceilings make moving pictures on the white tile floor, an irresistible siren song calling all toddlers to spin and dance. Candy kiosks with counters set at the height of a four-year-old have assorted bowls of colored sugar and come equipped with shovels. The Disney Store. Full stop. There are flat screen TVs at the deep end of all the children's clothing stores, mesmerizing tiny brains with cartoons. All to make it easier on the parents so they can stay longer and buy more.

"It's very clever," Ally says. "When I was a kid, I used to get an orange Julius as a reward if I behaved. Now I have to drag Lucy out of there – past the indoor playground."

"So, there have been some improvements on childhood after all," I say, referencing a darker conversation Ally and I had the other day. She rolls her eyes.

"When do you go back?" Juliet asks me.

"Tomorrow." I'll be grateful to get home and relax, truth be told. After a week, I'll miss everyone again, though. That's how it always goes. Their lives go on without me and I miss so much from one summer to the next.

Ally's looking past me. "There are people with champagne." She stands up, scanning the room. "No waiters with trays. I'm going to the bar. Want one?"

In college, I took a certain pride in my tolerance for alcohol, but now I don't even drink on New Year's Eve.

She waves away my look of uncertainty. "You don't have to

drink the whole thing." She looks under the table for the shoes she slipped off as soon as we got here. She finds one, scrunches her nose, and decides to go barefoot.

When I told my parents I wanted to move to Tucson, they were understandably confused. It didn't help that I couldn't really explain it, at least not all of it.

They had just begun to settle into having me close by again. When I'd chosen New York for college, they'd been vocal about their dismay, only somewhat appeased by my returning for Christmas and summer breaks. Their assumption that my homecoming was a permanent and settled fact was abundantly clear.

We had many discussions at the dining room table that ended with my mother leaving in tears, my father sighing and shaking his head. In the end, they relented and helped me make the move across the country. My mother stayed with me that first week to help get me settled and be sure I felt confident on my own. I had grown up a happily spoiled only child, a daughter, and it was hard to say how much my diagnosis was a part of that. In some ways, I'm sure it made them more overprotective, but in other ways they were more accommodating. Anything I chose to do with my life was ultimately better than the worst-case-scenario the doctors had given them. They found my liberal politics adorable, my pretentious, perplexing comparative literature major irrelevant to the fact that I was a college graduate. If I had to go away to college, wanted to try out life in a desert, they would grin and bear it. They'd learned they could bear almost anything.

Sometimes I wondered if they ever wished they'd had a second child. It felt especially cruel that I was their only shot. If they'd had two kids, they'd still have a chance at all those social milestones: weddings and grandbabies and bragging to friends about that big promotion.

If this was something they thought, they were kind enough not to admit it.

Ethan makes the rounds among the guests, arriving at our table last. "My single ladies table" he calls it.

"I'm an old married lady!" Ally protests.

Ethan shrugs. He has lost his bow tie somewhere along the

journey. He's been dancing. Even with the top two buttons of his shirt undone and the autumn cross-breeze, his forehead shines under the twinkly lights. "You came as Sara's date so I assumed you had an arrangement."

I put my arm around Ally. "You're due a night off."

"I'll let you explain that to my husband when someone posts a photo of me making out with a groomsman," Ally says.

"Good luck finding a groomsman drunk enough to make out with a girl," Ethan fires back and the table erupts in laughter.

Ethan sits in the empty chair beside me. Some of the women from our table have moved to the dance floor. Across from me, the gallery owner with white hair has spent most of the evening looking at her iPhone. Three more have turned their chairs to watch the dancing. When the other women left, Juliet said she couldn't possibly dance, blamed her shoes.

"So, do you feel totally different now?" Juliet asks.

Ethan considers this as he examines the simple silver band on his finger. "Not really," he says. "But it sure is fun to say that word: my *husband*." His body gives a little shake as if a chill has crept up his spine. "It's a better word. You know what I'm talking about." He nods at Ally.

She shrugs.

He rolls his eyes. "You just used it!" He pitches his voice higher, mocking. "'Explain it to my *husband*,' she says. You heteros have just learned to take it for granted."

Ally looks to me for defense. I just laugh and shake my head.

"Maybe it'll hit me tomorrow," Ethan says.

"I was kind of depressed the day after," Ally says and I scowl. I hadn't known about this. "It's like the letdown you feel the day after Christmas, but worse 'cuz there won't be another in a year. I was one of those girls who plans her wedding her whole life." She was. I remember being surprised when she didn't want the bridesmaid's dresses to be lavender because that's what had been decided when we were teenagers. "And then it's just over. That was it."

"If you're lucky." Ethan reaches for my water glass and helps himself. "I didn't grow up planning my wedding. This is mostly Colin." He waves an arm around the room. "I never expected this would be possible, so there's no letdown when it's over."

"I don't really believe marriage has an inherent value," Juliet says. "Just a social one. It only matters as far as whether it matters to other people."

I nod, but Ethan frowns, dubious.

"We only ever think things have value when we compare what we have to someone else," Juliet says. "It's why you see happy kids in third-world villages who don't know they're poor. I don't mean hunger, but other kinds of poverty. It's relative."

"My kids are like that," Ally says. She tells a story about Grace from our recent trip to the park. She'd been happy to play in the sandbox until she noticed another kid with a pail and a shovel.

"Right," Juliet says. "She defined her poverty in relation to her neighbor. It's the same with marriage." She turns to Ethan. "You only wanted it because it was something other people had. Which is fine, of course." Juliet laughs. "And congratulations." Her lips spread wide, showing slightly crooked teeth that somehow only add character to her otherwise generically perfect pretty face.

"You came to my beautiful wedding to tell me marriage is meaningless?" Ethan sneers, but there's no real malice in it.

Juliet laughs. "Sorry. My inner sociologist." She works at the admissions department at Mount Holyoke. "Anyway, not meaningless. Of course not. It has whatever meaning you decide to give it."

"So now that the gays can finally do it, the women are done getting married?" Ethan asks.

"Just some of us," I say.

"Juliet, too. Marcus has proposed every year on her birthday for the last . . . How many years now?"

Juliet flushes pink, but she answers. "Seven."

"Marriage isn't for everyone," Ally says, diplomatically.

My champagne glass is still nearly full. Ally's has one sip left. I lift hers. "But here's to everyone being able to decide for themselves."

We all agree we can drink to that. No one mentions the new right wing Supreme Court nomination, that precarious feeling in the air, as if naming it might jinx everything, break the spell. We celebrate into the wee hours, laughing into the abyss, daring the universe to pull the rug out from under our dancing feet.

In college, I listened to my friend's tales of heartbreak with some degree of envy. I believed with the earnestness of someone who'd never been in love that having your heart broken was an essential life experience. I argued some version of this to Ethan once, as part of my attempt to cheer him up after one of his romantic disasters. He'd lifted his head from my shoulder, wiped his tear-stained face, and laughed at me bitterly as if I were a stupid child.

A few years later, when my own heart was broken for the first and only time, I felt the same disgust for the idiot I'd once been. When I asked him how he'd managed not to throttle me back then, he simply squeezed my hand and welcomed me to the other side of the veil.

The first guy I dated after I moved to Tucson was a bit of a rebound pick. I fell hard and fast and thought he was amazing. He wasn't. A few months in, he began talking down to me, talking to me like I was stupid.

"I think he's gearing up to hit me," I told Ally over the phone, and I was only partly kidding.

"That's not funny," Ally said and I realized she was right.

I broke up with him by telling him we weren't in love with each other anymore, framing it as a realization we had both come to, but that only I had said out loud. Slowly, he agreed and mumbled something about staying friends. That was the last time we spoke. Over the next few years, this careful break up technique became my MO for slipping out of relationships that had run their course.

I can't imagine having that conversation with Tim. It makes as much sense as breaking up with Ally or Ethan or my parents. The family you choose is just as strong as the one you're born into. Sometimes stronger.

We stay until nearly midnight, knowing we have about an hour's drive back to the hotel. When Ethan hugs me goodbye, he gets a bit weepy.

"It's always magic when I get to see you," he says. "Magic."

"You and Colin need to come see me in Tucson, then."

I don't sleep in the car because I feel responsible for keeping Ally awake. I talk a blue streak and when I run out of things to say, I find a classic rock radio station and sing along, making up the lyrics I don't know.

We collapse into bed at my hotel in a fit of giggles as Ally mimics some of my sillier guesses.

"Knock it off. I'll have to pee," I tell her and she buries her laughter into her pillow.

She throws her arm across me. "I'm not ready for you to go home."

"I know, me neither. But I'll be back."

"Okay," she says and her arm turns to lead as she starts to snore.

Tim: Sunday

When I get up, Lola's waiting for me in the kitchen, standing over her empty food dish with a silent accusation. Now that she sees me, she begins her constant meowing, dancing at my feet as I prepare her breakfast, obviously not fast enough. She doesn't shut up until I set the dish on the tile.

Once she's satisfied, I begin to make my coffee. I've started my day this way for the last sixteen years, minus the ten months I was on my ride around the world. Finding someone to watch Lola while I was away was one of the trickiest parts of planning that trip. It wasn't like I was a complete loner, but I didn't have a lot of the type of friends you can ask that sort of favor from.

I ended up hiring a vet tech who worked at the place I'd taken Lola since she was a kitten. I asked if she had any ideas and she volunteered. I might have thought she was hitting on me, but she had an equality tattoo on the inside of her wrist and she gave off a certain vibe. I didn't know her well, but figured Lola couldn't do much better than a professional animal lover so I accepted immediately and gave notice to my employer. He let me know he wouldn't be holding my job while I was gone. I hadn't expected he would. I put a few things in storage, got Renee to pick up Lola (since I didn't have a car) and started west.

I felt pretty cocky when I left, like I was setting off on a journey that would be meaningful and intense and life-altering. And it was. I was in a hotel in Egypt the night Mubarak stepped down and the streets erupted in celebratory gun fire. I was smoking in the parking lot with a security guard who liked to bum American cigarettes. I'd been there for weeks while I waited for a visa and we'd struck up a sort of friendship. His English was better than my Arabic and I was surprised how we muddled through. Bakari laughed at me as I ducked behind a car when the gunshots started. Then we stayed up late into the night as he spoke of his fragile hopes for democracy. He was young enough that he couldn't remember a time when his country had any other leader. I tried to imagine thirty years of Nixon or Reagan or Clinton. I can complain all day about the United States government, but the fact that I struggled in that particular attempt makes me lucky.

Once my paperwork came through, I left Bakari a pack of Marlboros and my email address and tried to fit in as many miles before sundown as I could, just ready to be done. I blew past the pyramids and got on a boat across the Mediteranean, struck by how insignificant it was, how insignificant I was. By the end, I was worn out and homesick, but I wasn't sure what for. There was nothing much waiting for me in Tucson, nothing but Lola, and she was the only one I wanted to see when I got back. I called Renee and arranged to visit as soon as I returned (before I even had an apartment to take her to) and she let me know she'd be working, but her roommate would be happy to let me stop by.

When Sara opened the door, I assumed she was Renee's girlfriend. I hardly looked at her – a skinny girl with dirty blonde hair, in a wheelchair – desperate as I was for a familiar face.

"You must be Lola's person," she said and I agreed that I was.

Sara offered me a drink and I accepted as I'd learned to do on my trip. Never refuse hospitality. We sat in the living room.

"I just saw her using the litter box, so she's probably on her way to the kitchen for a snack. Speak of the devil," she said as Lola slunk around the corner.

Lola was indeed heading for the kitchen, but when she saw us, she changed course in her beeline and came toward us instead. She sniffed at my feet and as I bent to pat her, she slipped past me and hopped into Sara's lap. "Oooh, burn." Sara laughed, running a hand down Lola's back. "I think she likes me 'cuz I always have a lap available." She scratched Lola's chin and murmured to her. "I hope you know not to take it personal," she said, looking back up at me with a furrowed brow. "That's just cats. You were gone and she missed you. But she has to get even a little bit."

I did know that, of course, but it still hurt. Sara must have seen it on my face. She wheeled forward so that our knees were touching and kept talking. I was still getting used to conversations in English again, still hadn't shaved my traveling beard. Sara asked me questions about my trip and I struggled to form full sentences. I had never been much of a talker, but now my native language sounded strange coming out of my mouth.

While I was traveling, I'd learned key phrases to help me get by (*Can I have the check please? Where is the mechanic? Will someone call a doctor?*) but I didn't know enough to be fluent in any language but my own and after ten months, I'd grown hungry for conversation. But the moment it was presented to me, I faltered. The experience had been profound, it changed me, but I didn't know how to put it all into words.

Sara filled the gaps with chit-chat about the weather and politics and eventually Lola ventured across the bridge she'd made. Sara rolled backward as Lola curled into a ball on my lap. I cupped my palm over the warm, vibrating ball of her and I was home.

A few days later, once I'd rented an apartment, Renee brought Lola over and introduced me to her girlfriend, Cheryl. That's the day I asked for Sara's number, but I didn't call for several weeks. I had to get a job and a haircut and some furniture for my place.

And I had to figure out how a guy with a motorcycle dates a girl in a wheelchair. So far, that's been our biggest hurdle so I guess it was a problem worth solving.

This weekend's class is full up, like I told Delilah it would be. I'm assigned as coach number two, so Eddie takes the lead. This time, I sit in the folding chair while he unloads the bikes from the Conex.

Delilah had sounded sort of desperate on the phone. I remember that feeling, that kind of urgent search for meaning. It hit me suddenly at about the same age she's at now. Thirty-three? Thirty-four? I feel for her.

Sara just turned thirty-four this summer, but I've never known her to be uncertain or lost. She's steady as a rock, present in the moment, sure of herself.

Before we moved in together, we'd gone on a trip and they'd screwed something up with our reservation. We got it straightened out and as we were putting our bags in the room, Sara noted that she'd never seen me angry or flustered.

"You're so laid back, so calm," she said.

She was right about me. I wasn't faking it. But I hadn't always been this way. I'd been back from my trip for a year by then and that was the first time I noticed how much I'd changed. I cringe sometimes when I remember the guy I used to be: short-tempered and directionless and insecure. Sara never would have taken a second look at that guy, no matter the clean shave.

That's what I recognized in Delilah. That silent, jittery panic. I think I saw it that first day, how uncomfortable she is in her own skin. She's in the middle of it, you know, that thing they used to call mid-life crisis, except some of us have more than one and they come at different times.

I wonder if Sara will ever have one. I guess it's possible she had hers before we met but it's hard to imagine.

She'll figure it out, Delilah. Some of us have affairs or move across the country. Some of us need to spend the better part of a year with no one to talk to but ourselves. It's different for everyone.

At the lunch break, I eat some Slim Jims and head to CVS to look for a birthday card. My dad turns sixty-five on Thursday. Picking out a card for your father is hard for everyone, but I imagine it's harder when you haven't seen the guy in over twenty years. The "you're my role model" cards are all too much, but the ones joking about age seem too casual. "Wishing I could be there on your special day" seems dishonest. The blank cards require more than I'm prepared to give. There's a strange prevalence of golfing or fishing or hunting themed cards, none of which my father is particularly involved in, as far as I know.

One year I came across a card that started out with something like: "Even though we don't see eye to eye . . ." Why would you even get a card for the guy if that's the kind of relationship you have? Greeting cards are hardly the place to be honest about how little you care about someone. That's a waste of a stamp.

I skip over the Christian section. I don't even know if my dad believes in God. I don't know if I do. Sometimes I think about my mother looking down on me and whether she'd like what she sees, but I'm not sure that means I believe she's doing it. I think it's more of a what if scenario, a hypothetical.

Most of the time, it's just really basic stuff. Whenever Sara and I go to the opera, I wonder if my mother would like it as much as I do. She always liked Romeo and Juliet and all the shows seem like variations of that. Aida and Tosca. The idea that it's only true love if the lovers kill themselves at the end.

Sometimes it's about my life choices. Would Mom like Tucson? In February. Would she approve of Sara? Probably. What would she think about me never visiting my father?

I sigh. I read a slew of cards with cartoon animals on the front. If my mom were alive, I'd visit. Rooms were never quiet with her in them, even when she was sick.

After twenty minutes, I settle for one with a photo of three fat cats on the front. Inside it says: "Two out of three cats agree that you should do nothing for your birthday." It's so stupid and it only seems stupider as the day goes by and I can't stop thinking about it. The only reason I choose it instead of the many other equally stupid options is that one of the cats reminds me of the one I'd had as a kid. Marmalade. I don't even remember if my dad liked that cat, or cats in general. I don't know if he'll make the connection.

It's horrible, but it's the only thing that gets me out of the store and back to the range on time.

Eddie likes to hear himself talk and class runs way over. The sun is setting while we're finishing up the exam, which is not particularly safe or professional. I make a mental note to avoid coaching with Eddie in the future. I have to rush home to get the car so I can pick Sara up at the airport.

I park in the garage and meet her in baggage claim. She spots me first because I'm tall and when I locate her, she's already grinning.

"Hey mister, can I get a ride?" she asks.

"It'll cost you," I reply and I lean down to kiss her.

On the drive home, we pass the remnants of a motorcycle accident. The lights of the cop car blink red in the darkness. The police are still there, but the rider is gone. Just the bike laying on its side, broken glass sparkling in the flashing light.

"Do you recognize the bike?" Sara asks as we pass the wreckage.

"It's too dark."

"Do you want to turn around?"

I don't answer. I know she's had a long day in airports. She just wants to go home.

"It's fine, babe," she says, reaching out to touch the back of my neck.

I ease the car into the middle lane, swing down a side street and turn around in a wide circle.

"I'll just be a minute," I say as I step from the car.

She gives me a quick nod and pulls out her cell phone to signal that she'll be checking her email and is in no rush.

As I approach the officers, I introduce myself. "I'm a rider coach, so I know a lot of the bikers in town. Thought I might recognize the bike." I look it over. It's a Harley with high, arched handlebars. Those of us who don't ride Harleys call them "ape hangers". I've never understood how that could be comfortable, how your hands wouldn't go numb from the bad circulation. I don't know any Harley riders personally. The bike is not familiar.

"How's the rider?" I ask.

The officer shakes his head at me. "Not at liberty to say."

I nod. What a prick. Like he can't say whether the guy went to the morgue or the hospital. The mirrors are broken and the brake lever's twisted, but if he was wearing his gear, he'd be okay. Unfortunately, a lot of these guys opt for the pirate costume: the leather vest instead of shoulder armor and elbow pads, the acid wash jeans instead of Kevlar or leather pants that protect bare skin from road burn, the do-rag instead of a helmet.

"You gotta have a death wish to ride one of these things," the officer says without looking up from his clip board. "It's just a matter of time."

There's no point in arguing with him. I lift my hand and wave. "Have a good night."

I walk back to the car and Sara smiles at me through the windshield.

As I slide in behind the steering wheel, she fans herself with my dad's birthday card. "Two out of three cats, eh?"

"I know. It's awful, isn't it?"

"Dad cards are the worst."

Sara: Monday

I'm making the grocery list at the computer when Tim tells me that while I was away, he watched a documentary on the sustainability of cattle farming and has decided to give up red meat. He says he doesn't expect me to give it up, but if we're going to continue eating meals together, I know what that means. We already don't eat a lot of red meat – another documentary on factory farming and my lack of empathy for chicken and fish have accomplished that.

"We're becoming those people," I say. We no longer eat most brand name chocolate because of an article I read about child labor, neither of us have a smart phone because of the thing in the Congo and I use biodegradable K-cups in the coffee machine my mother bought us last Christmas – even though we don't do gifts. We gave up cable and get our news off the internet, which is probably for the best, really. I refuse to buy clothing from sweat shops, and since I can't afford $300 jeans, this mostly means I shop at thrift stores or not at all. My collection of sexy underwear has suffered the most.

Tim stands behind me and rubs my shoulders. "I know." He reads the list I'm making. "How about some *shrimps*?" he suggests, hopefully.

"Expensive," I grumble. I have trouble justifying anything that costs more than nine dollars a pound. Once it gets into double digits, it's out of bounds. I type "chicken drumsticks, ground turkey, tilapia."

When I moved out on my own after college, I ate tuna casserole and hamburger helper. I had dinner with my parents once a week – and it wasn't for the conversation. The cost of living is one of the reasons I moved here. My mortgage for a three-bedroom house in a community with an HOA is half what rent was back east for a one-bedroom apartment in a crappy neighborhood.

It's so much cheaper to live in Tucson. Even living off social security, I've managed to feel pretty flush for the past few years, splitting the bills with a roommate. I can even afford a Netflix membership. I add "shrimp?" and Tim pumps his fist in the air.

I go into the kitchen to take stock of what we have in the fridge. On the refrigerator door, there's every condiment you can think of, but the rest of it is pretty bare. The veggie drawer is empty. The deli drawer has half a bag of shredded Mexican cheese. What has he been eating while I've been gone?

On the top shelf, I see a carton of eggs, two sticks of butter and half a can of cat food. They're up high because I'm not meant to reach them. As far as Lola's concerned, I don't know how to use a can opener and am of very little practical use to her. I think it's part of the reason she doesn't acknowledge me as an authority figure. She would never think of jumping on the counter when Tim's around, but I have to yell my head off before she hops down again. I'm just good for a cuddle.

There's still half a gallon of milk with an expiration date of tomorrow and something unidentifiable in a Tupperware container at the back. If I lived alone, I'd just throw the entire container in the trash to spare myself the smell of the contents. But Tim would rinse it out and recycle. If he sees it in the trash, he'll pull it out, shake his head at me.

Living with someone means being accountable for who you really are. You can't pretend to be that better version of yourself – the one who wakes up with minty breath and great hair, never gets impatient, always does the right thing. After those first few months, the myth crumbles. He farts and blames the cat. I spill dinner down my shirt and don't bother to change it. There's no bullshit; you're seen.

As I weigh my options, the container sits. It has already been in there for months

I moved to Tucson because I was running away. No one really knows the whole story. They all thought I was being adventurous and brave. They still think that. They have no idea.

It's true that I didn't know anyone when I came here. There's certainly something intimidating about that and making adult friends and building a new life from scratch can be daunting.

But I didn't really do that, at least not right away.

Besides the cost of living and the weather, the main reason I picked Tucson is that it had grocery delivery. It allowed me to hide out and be accountable to no one.

Those first few months, I hardly went anywhere beyond the small, fenced-in, dirt patio behind my apartment. I didn't make friends. I wasn't brave or adventurous. I used a cane on weekly trips to get the mail, in the middle of a weekday when it was unlikely I'd run into anyone. I sent emails with made-up stories about the book club I had joined, the painting class, how I was volunteering at the Y.

I was full of these stories when I went home for Ally's wedding that October. Only one person knew I was lying. Ethan had flown in for the weekend and we only had the briefest of moments alone together at the reception.

I don't remember what I said. I was speaking breezily through a numbing haze caused by not enough sleep and too much champagne.

He squeezed my upper arm until I winced and looked him in the eye. "Stop being full of shit," he said. "That was not our deal."

Before I could protest, the crowd pressed in on us again and pulled us in different directions, in that confusing chaos of wedding physics.

When I got back to Tucson, I tried harder. I figured out how to use the city paratransit and started taking weekly trips to Target or my local library. I began the long process of getting my health insurance to cover my very first wheelchair. It was surprisingly therapeutic to yell and cry at the insurance agents over the phone.

I learned to drive that chair on the paved paths of my apartment complex. I met neighbors going to the mail room or hanging out by the pool. And when I met people, I didn't have to explain. I didn't have to take on anyone else's surprise or disappointment or sorrow.

That was the real gift of moving someplace where nobody knew me. What seems frightening to other people was actually freeing. The burden of other people's expectations had lifted. I don't even think I'd understood the weight of it until I realized it was gone.

I made some of my lies true. I met my friend Renee at a book club meeting. *Atonement*. Everyone kept talking about Kiera Knightly. I think we might have been the only two people who actually read the book. We stayed in the back of the store after the meeting dispersed talking about that nasty little girl who'd ruined everything, Briony. We agreed to see the movie together at the cheap theater that weekend. Neither of us went back to that book club, but we kept in touch.

Renee was funny in a sarcastic, deadpan way. She gave a tough first impression, but was actually very sensitive. She was a vet tech without any pets. When I asked how that happened, she confided that her ex-girlfriend had taken the dog when she moved away. Renee was dating again, but still too heartbroken to get another dog.

By the time my lease was up, we decided to move in together, to a bigger place, closer to downtown. When I went home in August, I was stronger. I had been brave and adventurous. I had built something real.

"Mmm, what's that smell?" I say, as we pass through the door to David's kitchen.

"Sadie made lasagna," David says. He pats her shoulder and she slouches against the counter by the oven.

"Lasagna, Sadie? I'm impressed."

"It's not that hard," she says, and she bends to hug me hello. She's so tall. When I look at her, I still see the freckled, frizzy-haired twelve-year-old she was when I met her, but she has long since discovered flat irons and foundation. The versions of her blur together and it's hard for me to imagine what the rest of the world sees. It must be even harder for David.

Tim hands David a bottle of beer, takes one for himself and puts the rest in the fridge. We take our seats around the large round table at the far end of the kitchen. It's set with square blue plates and a basket of garlic bread in the center. David makes a joke of taking credit for that part of the meal. Tim sits on my right and Sadie's on my left. David is hesitating between the remaining two places when Delilah comes in behind me. I know because he looks up and says her name. I turn.

Delilah's dark curls are pulled into a ponytail. She wears a long skirt, silver hoop earrings and no make-up. Somehow, she's a bit more Bohemian than I was expecting, though I'm not sure why I was expecting anything or what it would have been.

David walks to her side and makes formal introductions. We shake hands and I'd swear she's frowning at me at first, except that would be weird. She blinks and smiles, but it's a smile I don't totally trust and I don't know why.

"Anybody want wine?" she asks and when there are no takers, she flits to the cabinet and retrieves a single glass.

The oven timer beeps and while David carries the lasagna to the table, Delilah takes the chair on the other side of Tim.

It turns out the lasagna is vegetarian. Sadie and Delilah have seen the same documentary. Delilah was the one who recommended it to Tim. The two of them discuss it for most of the dinner while Sadie tells me what she's reading. I can't get over how little assigned reading lists have changed since I was in school. Surely someone has created something worth reading in the past twenty years. David keeps checking his phone. Eventually, the conversations come together and we go around the table declaring our favorite books.

Sadie just finished *Everything I Never Told You.*

"For school or for pleasure?" I ask.

"For pleasure."

I raise my eyebrows, thinking of her heavy work load. This is her senior year and she has college applications to worry about.

"That's my girl," David says proudly. His choice is *The Lord of the Rings* and he shrugs, unperturbed, when Sadie calls him a geek.

"*The Poisonwood Bible,*" Delilah says.

"I love Barbara Kingsolver," I say. "I've read all her books."

"Have you read that one, Sadie?" Delilah asks.

Sadie squints at the ceiling and scrunches her nose. "Doesn't sound familiar."

Delilah folds her arms across the table and turns to Tim. "How about you?"

"*Ishmael.* Sara made me read it. It's totally weird. The premise? It's, like, a talking gorilla."

"What?" Sadie looks at me, laughing. I nod.

"But it really makes you think," he says.

"About what?"

"About human civilization. How we have fucked everything up, basically."

"Sounds depressing," David says.

"It's not, though. It's just realistic, no sugar coating." Tim puts his hand on my thigh under the table, gives it a squeeze. "Right?"

I shrug. It had depressed me a bit, but I found some hope in it, too.

Delilah pulls out her phone. "I gotta write it down or I'll forget."

Everyone else at the table looks at me. "Last one," Tim says. "Make it good."

That night, Tim and I sit in bed with our Kindles.

"Whatcha reading?" I ask.

"The new one from the guy who wrote *Fight Club*."

"What tense is it?"

He has to look. "Present."

"Do you know some people get cranky about present tense?"

"I do know that," he says. "It is known. I am knowing it."

I smile. Lola jumps up on the bed and I startle. She gets me every time, so quiet on the approach. She climbs onto my chest, forcing me to put my reading aside to scratch her chin. "Do you know how long Delilah's staying?"

"No." Tim sighs. "David's worried she's a bad influence on Sadie. Got her talking about joining the Peace Corps, putting off college."

"The Peace Corps? Jesus, I can't imagine. Little Sadie in a third world country. Didn't she just get her braces off?"

Tim snickers at me. Lola jumps down. She'll go get a snack in the kitchen and return in an hour or so to curl up near Tim. He's her favorite. "I told David to go easy on her," he says. "Delilah. I think she's going through something. She seems a little, I don't know, what did you think?"

"I thought she seemed to have a crush on you."

He blows a raspberry.

"I don't blame her. I have a crush on you, too. You're very crushworthy."

And then we're kissing. I was too tired for sex last night, but I've been thinking about it all day. Sex with Tim is one of my favorite things about being alive.

David: Tuesday

When Sadie and I leave the house in the morning, Delilah still isn't awake. She didn't get up in time to see us off yesterday either and I'm trying to pretend it has nothing to do with the fight we had Friday morning. Even calling it that seems dishonest, as if we were equal participants when really it was just me yelling at her while she looked baffled and, frankly, a little bit afraid.

We've been carefully polite with each other since. I guess we've agreed to pretend it never happened. I probably should have apologized, though I'm not sure I'm sorry.

"I guess she's adjusted to the time change," I say brightly and Sadie says nothing in response. She hitches her backpack on her shoulder as the garage door groans open and looks at her fingernails in a way that suggests she's not buying it.

I press the clicker, unlocking the car, and Sadie climbs inside. For the first half of the drive, I pepper her with superficial questions about the school's basketball team and her friend Margot as she leans her head back against the seat rest and answers me with her eyes closed.

I take a breath and pause for three beats. "Do you need any help with your college essays?"

"Nope." She says it so fast I can't tell whether it's a *nope - got it covered* or *nope - not writing any.*

Sadie hasn't said anything more about putting off college for a year and I'm sort of afraid to mention it. If she's dropped the idea on her own, it may be better not to make an issue of it. I don't want her to pursue it just to prove a point.

As a sophomore, Sadie went to Costa Rica with her Spanish class. I'd encouraged her to go. It would be a great experience and look good on her college applications. While she was away, Paris was attacked by terrorists and I started reading articles online about the Costa Rica government, their drug policies and violent crime statistics. One writer pointed to a "spike" in crime that indicated a "pandemic" that was likely related to the drug cartels wreaking havoc in Honduras and Guatemala. Why hadn't I read these articles before I let her go?

By the time she came home, safe and sound thank God, my view of the world had changed. The Mexican border was an hour away, but I kept Sadie's passport in a lockbox with important papers. Heck, even Europe wasn't safe. What were the chances the Peace Corps would station her in Scottsdale?

I don't talk about my job much. For one thing, I can't. I'm an engineer for a defense contractor and that's all I can say. Which is fine with me. It's a touchy subject for some people, and you can't always tell who.

At the last Fourth of July barbeque, Sara went off on a rant about how the US spends more on national defense than the next eight countries combined. And we're more likely to be hit by lightning than killed by a terrorist. See, I happen to think these things are connected and whatever that level of safety costs, I'm happy to pay the price. I'm secretly proud to be part of the military industrial complex.

For the rest of the ride, we're quiet as all I can think of are things I've decided not to say out loud. I park at the curb and Sadie leans in to kiss my cheek in that thoughtless blur of routine. I'm wishing her a good day as the door closes behind her.

I'd left Maryanne early on Saturday and snuck back into my house. Delilah's door was shut and by the time we crossed paths, after I'd showered and changed clothes, she never asked when I'd come home. Sadie returned from her friend's house after lunch and spent most of the day in her room, doing homework.

I spent the weekend trying to hide my Cheshire cat grin, deciding not to send flowers, forcing myself not to text her. I didn't want to seem overeager. When I broke down and called her Sunday night, I got her voicemail, left a rambling message and hoped she'd call back anyway.

She hasn't.

So now I'm pretty sure I blew it. I've gone back over it a thousand times and I don't think it could have been that night or else why would she have asked me to stay? It must have been something I said or did the next morning. Or something I didn't say or do that I should have. Maybe the instinct to send flowers had been right after all. Maybe it wouldn't have felt like too much because who has time for wishy-washy anymore? Maybe at this stage of life, it's serious inquiries only.

Or maybe it didn't mean that much to her. She got what she wanted and she's moving on down her list, getting her money's worth out of that dating membership. It's 2017 and women don't have to be shy about their sexual needs, confusing orgasms with emotions.

Maybe I'm the one stuck in the past in that department.

Years ago, I'd pretty much given up on sex. I thought Janet and I had a sexless marriage, but it turned out I was the only one going without. When she confessed her affair, I was surprised but it didn't hit me the way I would have expected. I didn't feel jealous or betrayed, just sad. It certainly shocked me out of my status-quo complacency and I filed for divorce. It turned out our love hadn't just evolved to a different place where physical intimacy was unnecessary; it was gone.

She'd been fucking a married man and they made a pact to tell their spouses. His wife had a different reaction, though. She forgave him and they recommitted to their union. By the time my divorce was finalized, Janet was living with her mother and her lover was welcoming a new baby into his life.

I wonder sometimes if we could have done that. I didn't think there had been anything to rekindle, but maybe I had kicked dirt on the dying embers when they really needed someone to cup their hands around them and offer a gentle last breath. We could have a six-year-old now.

Mostly, that thought just makes me tired.

In my office, I set my phone on my desk. I swipe the screen. No messages. I read through the old texts to be sure I haven't missed anything, but it's still the same conversation that I read this morning and last night, the one we had before meeting up Friday for dinner.

Tim and I don't usually do lunch during the week, but I'm feeling desperate. When I text him the address of a diner about half-way between us, he replies immediately: "I'm there."

The accuracy of that statement makes me choke up. I remember how welcoming he was when I'd show up to that brew pub Wednesday nights after my divorce. He'd tell me to pull up a chair, always seeming happy to see me. It must have been obvious to him how lost I was.

I shake my head clear of the memory. I've got to get it together.

I scroll through the calendar on my phone. Thanksgiving is next month. We'll probably go to Tim and Sara's place. Sara's mom makes a turkey; we bring pie. It's been the tradition for several years running.

The last time I went home for Thanksgiving, Sadie was a baby. That was the only time Sadie went with me to New Hampshire, the only time she and Delilah ever met before this year. My mother came out to visit a few times, but I remember those weeks as so stressful. Janet was convinced my mother didn't like her and despite her careful politeness, I wasn't sure I disagreed. There was no warmth between them. Perhaps my mother recognized in Janet something I had yet to find.

When my mother passed away, Sadie cried, but it had been three years since they'd seen each other and three years is an eternity to a child. I'd known it was coming, had visited a few weeks before, but that loss wrecked me. I still have a hard time thinking about it and prefer to imagine her puttering around the house I grew up in as if it has just been a few months since we've talked instead of years.

"She's a bitch."

"I'm not sure she is." I run my hand through my hair. Is it getting thinner? Every time I get a haircut, I think my hairline seems further back.

"If she doesn't see what a good catch you are, who needs her?"

"But maybe it's just a miscommunication. Should I call her?"

"Again?" Tim look up from his menu with raised eyebrows. "No."

"But how will I know what happened?"

"You won't." He closes his menu and lays it flat on the table, his hands on top. "You'll never know. There's a whole world of information you never had access to. There could be another guy you never knew you were competing with or she may have suddenly decided she's not ready after all. You'll drive yourself crazy trying to figure it out."

He's trying to caution me against doing this, but the way he's put it seems prophetic and I think: *Yes, I will. I will drive myself crazy!*

The waitress comes over and Tim orders a grilled cheese and fries, but I get a bacon cheeseburger because who knows the next time I'll see red meat as long as Sadie and Delilah are on their cowless kick.

"Do you know how long Delilah is staying?"

"It feels rude to ask."

"She showed up out of the blue and hasn't mentioned how long she plans to stay?"

I nod. When he puts it like that, it sounds unreasonable.

"Have you figured out what she's running away from?"

"Nope. When I asked about the bruise on her face, she said it wasn't what I thought." I reach for my soda. "But I've heard that before."

Tim looks up as he's pouring sugar into his iced tea. "You have?"

"My mother."

Tim's face tightens into a grimace. "Sorry, man. I didn't realize."

I shrug like it's nothing. I've never told Tim about this. It's not like we don't talk about serious subjects. My divorce, my worries for Sadie. But my father has never come up. It helps that he's dead.

"Do you think Delilah's repeating a pattern she learned in childhood?"

"That's what's weird. My dad was sober by the time she was born. I was always under the impression she hadn't known any of that."

Tim leans back in the booth and scowls. "Well, maybe you should talk to her about it," he says, crossing his arms. "She strikes me as a person who needs someone to talk to."

When I get home, Delilah's car isn't parked on the curb, highlighting another change for this week: she's not cooking dinner anymore.

In the kitchen, Sadie has homework spread across the large table.

"Did you see Delilah before she left?"

"Nope."

"Getting hungry?"

"Yep."

I pull a bag out of the freezer and get the skillet out of the cabinet.

"Whatcha workin' on?"

"Algebra."

I always loved algebra in school. It's like puzzles. I don't think it comes as easily for Sadie, but she still gets As.

I stand at the stove with a spatula as Sadie hunches over her work.

"She didn't leave a note or anything?"

"Huh?"

"Delilah."

"Not that I know of."

I turn down the burner and give a quick look around the house. Nothing. I pull out my phone and check for messages.

It's just as well. I shouldn't have let myself get used to having her around. She could decide to leave at any moment. This thought makes me turn down the hallway and check the guest room. Her things are still here.

Relieved, I return to the kitchen. Of course she wouldn't leave without saying goodbye.

Delilah: Wednesday

When Sadie comes home from school, she stands in the bathroom doorway and watches as I do my hair.

"Wow," she says and she comes to stand next to me in front of the mirror.

"Too big?" My curls can not be contained within the vanity frame.

"No, you look fabulous."

"I spent years trying to force my hair straight, but eventually you learn to work with what you've got." I give my head a good shake. These days my confidence rises and falls in relation to how big my hair is.

"I think we have the same chin," Sadie says and I look closer at our reflections. We have a lot of the same things: the dark eyes and dark hair, hers artificially straightened. The angular chin, yes. The mouth: full bottom lip, thin top lip.

I tip my head against hers. "I think you're right." She could be mine.

Of course, not really. I'm much too young. But if I had a daughter, she might grow up to look like this.

"Can I come with you?" Sadie asks.

"It's a school night. I don't think your dad would approve."

She pouts and I'm relieved to make David be the bad guy. For what I have in mind for this evening, Sadie would really cramp my style.

"Have you guys made up?"

I shrug. "We're fine," I say. We managed not to see each other much this weekend, which is odd since I'm supposedly visiting him. I did some sightseeing on my own, driving to the top of Mt Lemmon where it was in the low seventies and smelled like home. I walked around a mostly deserted campground and ended up taking a nap in the pine needles.

Sadie pulls a basket of make-up from the cabinet under the sink. "You should move here." She hands me a lipstick.

"I should?" I remove the lipstick from its case and wind it up. The name on the bottom is Movie Star Mauve.

She continues to rifle through the basket, selecting her own color. "There are plenty of people in Tucson you could save."

I laugh. "That's true, I guess." I lean closer to the mirror and apply the color to my bottom lip. "Social workers are one of those things. We're needed everywhere, but do we really make a difference anywhere?" My lips press together and apart with a pop. It leaves some extra color in the divot at the middle of my top lip. I dab at it with my pinky.

"That's depressing." Sadie sits down on the closed toilet. "You don't really feel that way, do you?"

I sigh at my reflection. "Sometimes." There's just too many things wrong with the world. Bank fraud, climate change, hungry children, dying bees. I could devote my life to any of them and never make a dent. I already have.

"What do you care?" I ask. "You won't even be here. You'll be half-way around the world, right?"

She smiles and I see her getting more comfortable with the idea. It's becoming less fantasy, more something she can actually make happen. "That's next year. You should move here now." She approaches the mirror, spreads the lipstick on her bottom lip and presses her lips together. She uses her pinky to remove the bit of color from the divot in her top lip, just like me.

I take a seat at the bar and order a beer. I'm wearing my tightest jeans with a button-up plaid shirt I've only buttoned up part of the way. I even let Sadie do the rest of my make-up, but the lipstick comes off on the beer glass and the lights are too dim to see anything else.

I count two cowboy hats, but otherwise the pub is a lot more modern industrial hipster than the desert honkytonk cliché I was expecting.

When my cell phone rings, I pull it from my back pocket and look at the screen. I recognize the 603 area code, but not the number. It rings three times before I answer.

"Do you know where Marty is?"

"Uh?" In the mirror behind the fancy liquor bottles, I catch myself making a screwed-up face for the benefit of no one. "Who is this?"

"I'm just looking for Marty."

"Yeah. I got that." And then, knowing full-well who I'm talking to, I say again: "Who is this?"

There's a pause and I feel more powerful with every passing silent second. In this moment, I do not feel the shame of what I did to her car. It feels justified. I feel entitled to any amount of suffering I can squeeze out of her.

"Lyndsy," she says quietly and I think I can hear what it has cost her. I almost feel sorry for her. Almost.

I laugh. She's lost track of him already and she thinks he's with me. "Should I give him a message from you?"

"I just want to know that he's okay." Her tiny, scared voice takes all the *fun* out of the fun I'm having. How old is she?

I finish my beer and signal the bartender for another. "Look, I'm in Arizona. I have no idea where Marty is."

"Oh. Okay." She doesn't sound relieved. She doesn't hang up either.

"Is that all?" I snap.

"Um. Well. Can I ask you something?"

I lean my elbows on the bar in front of me and bow my head, eyes closed. "Why not?"

"Does Marty have a—" I hear her take a breath. "A drinking problem?"

Well, that was a short honeymoon. It's probably not a sign of maturity or mental health that I take some degree of pride in this. I'd distracted Marty from his addiction for months. The young blonde with the super long legs has barely had him to herself for a couple weeks.

"I mean, he's always been a partier," she's saying as the bartender replaces my empty glass with a full one and I mouth a *thanks*. "But. It used to just be a weekend thing."

That's when I remember it's Wednesday. I let a long silence swell as I consider whether I'll answer. "If he's getting drunk mid-week, it's gotten worse," I say.

"The thing is. It's not just booze."

That surprises me and I drift back in time, trying to remember if he'd given me any reason to suspect drug use. Poor Marty. What the hell does he have to be so unhappy about? College educated, otherwise healthy, straight, white, American man with a pretty young girlfriend. The world is his fucking oyster. I'm not really listening as Lyndsy tells me about the pills she found and the fight they had.

I cut her off. "Not to be a bitch, but this isn't really my problem."

She starts crying then and apologizing. It's not that I don't care, but I don't have it in me to walk her through this. It used to frustrate me when Marty and I were together. What sort of troubles was he drinking away? Why did he need to be so numb?

I take a long swig of my drink and steel myself. "If you're smart, you won't let it be your problem anymore either." And I hang up.

I'm nearly finished with my second beer when I see Tim come through the door. I let him be the one to notice me just so there's no sense that I followed him. David mentioned he comes here on Wednesdays, but so what? I was here first.

He's standing right next to me at the bar before he sees me. When he says my name, I turn and feign surprise. We hug hello. I close my eyes as I rest my head on his shoulder, holding him tight, breathing him in.

He pulls away. "What are you doing here?"

I tell him the story I practiced. I was driving by, recognized the name of the place. David had mentioned it.

"Oh yeah, he comes a lot in the summer." Tim comes all year. He usually just sits at the bar, but since I'm here, he suggests we get a table. "Have you eaten?"

As luck would have it, I have not. We move to a table in the corner and the waitress brings us menus. He orders a Red Cat Amber and I decide to give it a try. I don't even really like beer, but this isn't the kind of place where you can order a glass of wine without looking pretentious. They have twelve microbrews on tap.

We talk about our days. I went to the Desert Museum and have several funny anecdotes about desert creatures. The Prarie dogs popping up through the ground like Whack-a-Mole, the lizards as big as house cats. I skipped the exhibits on spiders because I prefer not to think about them. Tim works from home, but I notice he doesn't mention Sara when he recounts his day. I decide this is meaningful.

"Were you working as a programmer before you went on your trip?" I ask.

"Yep. I left my job when I decided to go."

"Scary?"

"Absolutely. I had to save up for a long time first. That's the catch-22 of the working man. Usually, if you're out of work, you can't afford to be going on trips. And when you have money, you're busy working."

"I hear that."

"I was thirty-five." He scratches his chin. "Have you noticed people always retire when they're too old to do anything fun? When you ride a motorcycle around the world, there are not nicely paved roads the whole way. No way I could have done it in my sixties. Hell, I'm already starting to feel those aches and pains."

I roll my eyes, smiling. He looks pretty fit to me. "How'd you get over oceans?"

"Boats." He says it like he's answering a silly question.

I giggle. "Of course."

The waitress brings our drinks and we both order the same salad. Another sign.

"So, do you like Tucson?"

I've been here for more than a week, but this is the first time I really think about it. What I like best are the mountains. They make me think I've never seen mountains before. Back home, they use the word for grassy hills. "I do. I'm sure the summers are brutal, though. How long have you lived here?"

"I moved here when I was eighteen."

"After your mom died?"

His eyes widen just the tiniest bit, as if he's surprised I made the connection, but he nods.

I picture him as a motherless boy, so young. "Are you close to your dad?"

"Not really." He leans back in his chair and looks up at the exposed rafters. I think this might be all he has to say. "His birthday's tomorrow. I'll call him, we'll have an uncomfortable ten-minute conversation and I'll check him off my list until Christmas. How about you?"

"My dad's dead."

"Oh yeah, sorry. I knew that. I keep forgetting you and David had the same parents."

"It's funny though. We kind of didn't." I run my finger around the edge of my glass. I'm trying to drink this one more slowly.

"How do you mean?"

"I was so much younger. I think their parenting style had really changed by the time I was born." I use the condensation on my fingertip to trace my initials on the table. On an empty stomach, those first two beers hit harder than they would have otherwise. "Does David ever talk about our dad?"

Tim shakes his head, but I'm not sure he'd tell me one way or the other. He seems too loyal.

"I remember when your mom passed. He was really broken up about it."

The food comes then and we do less talking. This is better than the meal I ate in my car last night. I've never been comfortable eating dinner alone in a restaurant, but I'm done cooking in David's big kitchen and I decided the clearest way to send that message was to be gone when he got home from work.

It had been fun that first week – looking up recipes and shopping for ingredients. Playing little Suzie Homemaker. It had lost its appeal after David's red-faced tirade on Friday. Suddenly, I have better things to do, like sleep in and watch decorating shows on cable. David gets all the channels, which is such a waste since he's almost never home.

In the parking lot, Tim points out different features of the older bikes and I nod along.

"And this is me," he says when we get to the end of the row. His bike is black and chrome, Italian, from the seventies.

"Is this the one I get to ride when you teach me?" I step closer and run my hand along the leather seat.

"Nah. My other bike is probably better to learn on."

I turn to him and toss my hair over my shoulder. "Okay. Whatever you think is best." I lean against his bike and it starts to tip. Tim rushes forward to steady it and then puts his hands on my upper arms, steadying me.

He looks at me closely. "You okay to drive?"

I imagine him giving me a ride on the back of his bike, the wind in my hair.

I lay my hand on his shoulder. "You worried about me?"

He steps back and my arm falls like dead weight at my side. "I can Google numbers for cabs," he says, reaching for his phone.

Shame warms my face. "Oh, no. I'm fine. Really."

He smiles, relieved.

I get into my car and watch in the rearview mirror as he puts on his helmet and climbs on his bike. He lifts his arm to wave before he turns onto the main road. I continue to watch that spot in the mirror as the sky darkens, unable to look myself in the eye.

Ally: Thursday

By Thursday, it's decided.

"Well isn't that something," my mother says with such vehemence you'd think I had just announced my intention to abandon my children and join the circus or pursue a life of crime.

We're sitting in the living room of their condo. I made a lasagna for Karl's grandparents and left it in the oven for the visiting nurse to take out when she arrives. They'll eat dinner, go to bed and then they'll be on their own until the homecare arrives in the morning. It'll be like this another week before Karl and I move in. The timetable has sped up and I have no idea how to get all that packing done. I haven't even been back to my apartment yet; I came straight here.

I go into some detail on Grammy's Alzheimer's, what kind of care she needs.

"Well that's so nice, what you're willing to do for his family."

I sit forward. "And what's that supposed to mean?"

My mother fusses over her hair, the same style she's had for thirty years. She presses the edges with the tips of her fingers; it doesn't move. "We're getting older and older and you keep moving further and further away," she says.

I remember watching her spray her hair with Aquanet when I was a kid, filling the bathroom with that sharp, metallic odor. Do they still sell aerosol spray? They must; her 'do maintains the same height as always. She did finally stop dyeing it that deep magenta that hadn't fooled anyone.

"I guess you want us to be sure not to count on you for anything," my mother says.

"Ma, I'm here every week. What do you need?"

She fiddles with the chain that holds her glasses around her neck. "Well, I never ask you for anything," she says, and she's not even trying to be sarcastic. "But, look at your father."

I turn. My dad is sitting in the green armchair with Lucy on his lap. She's wearing her ladybug costume from Halloween. She insisted on it this morning and I hadn't been able to think of a reason why not. My parents would get a kick out of it, I knew. The red tights and polka-dotted leotard. I'd made the wings out of wire and colored Saran Wrap. The antenna is a headband with pipe cleaners; Lucy calls them her "ears." Probably because last year she was a cat with little black triangles on a headband. My designs aren't fancy, but I don't believe in store-bought costumes or store-bought birthday cakes. Spending that extra time is the whole reason I had kids. That's what a happy life is made of.

My dad and Lucy are whispering to each other, having their own private conversation.

"Dad?"

He looks up as if only now remembering my presence.

"What's wrong with you?" I ask him.

"Nothing." He scowls. "Healthy as a horse."

"A horse!" Lucy squeals, giggling into her hands.

"That's not what the doctor said."

"Doctor?"

"Oh, hush, woman."

"What doctor?"

"Who wants a cookie?" My father's voice booms and my eyes dart nervously to the car seat where Grace sleeps soundly. She'd been crabby as we were leaving, but two minutes into the drive and she was zonked.

"I do, I do!" Lucy responds, surprising no one, and my father carries her off to the kitchen.

I look at my watch. Nearly dinner, but whatever. That's been my attitude lately. Pick your battles, that's what Sara always says.

I take a deep breath and look back at my mother.

It's like pulling teeth to get it all out of her, the bartering system of conversations with her that I'll never understand. For each nugget of information, I must pay with some groveling and a passive acceptance of her endless criticism of me. Of my weight, my skin, my parenting, my finances. Only after she has unburdened herself on these issues do I get the full picture: my father is having surgery to remove a tumor from his kidney on Monday. It was scheduled only days ago, but no one thought to call me.

I want to know which hospital he's going to and whether the surgeon has a good reputation. I'm not sure if they didn't ask any questions or if my mother just doesn't feel like sharing. My older brother already looked at the forms, she keeps saying, as if that should be the end of the conversation. He has no medical background, but he went to college (got a degree in business) and he's male so it makes perfect sense that they'd go to him.

I know what it means when doctors schedule surgery so quickly. It means they don't think there's time to dilly dally. My father has lived most of his life without health insurance. How long has that tumor been in there?

I go in the kitchen and tell him to sit down. He rolls his eyes, but humors me. I decide to have a cookie, too.

We leave before Grace wakes up. I buckle the girls in the backseat and pop a Disney sing-a-long into the tape deck for Lucy. When I stop to pick up Karl from work, I have no memory of the drive there.

I tell Sara first. That's how it's always been, even when I was pregnant with Lucy. Sara knew before Karl. We'd ordered daiquiris at a Mexican restaurant before I remembered. I had to call the waitress back to switch it to non-alcoholic and Sara's eyes bugged out of her head. I couldn't even keep a straight face.

So that time had sort of been an accident, but Sara's always been my go-to. I often don't know how I feel about something until I run it by her. Am I overreacting? And, on the other hand, what does it mean that I'm so numb right now?

"Shock?" she suggests over the phone. The girls are in bed and Karl fell asleep in front of the television. I've stretched out in the empty tub, with the door closed, keeping my voice low. The time difference works out for me in the evening. I can catch Sara before ten o'clock in Tucson.

"You think?"

"I don't know. You're the one studying to be a nurse." She laughs. "Maybe you've just gotten to the point where nothing fazes you."

"Maybe."

"You're going to be okay, though, whatever happens."

"I know." She doesn't tell me *it* will be okay because she can't promise that and she knows better than to pretend.

Sometimes I wonder if Sara and I would even be friends if we met today instead of in that art class when we were fourteen. Never mind that I can't imagine how we'd meet. The only people I meet these days are other parents or youngsters in my nursing class who decided what to be when they grew up before having kids.

"So, I start packing tomorrow," I say.

"Wow. You're really doing it."

"Yep." I know a big part of her thinks I'm crazy. It's not something she can even imagine doing.

It seems we have less in common with every passing year. At least, on the outside. She went to college and I didn't. I got married early and she thinks marriage is an outdated institution. She's never wanted kids, doesn't even particularly like them (though she swears she likes mine.) All of her Facebook posts are about politics while mine are shout-outs for kid's clothing sales. I suppose it's good that there are people who have time to worry about the world in the grand scheme of things. Right now, I'm just trying to get through the day.

"How did your mother take it?" she asks.

"As expected."

Sara groans.

On the inside, we're still the same people we were when we met, I think. And I'm grateful for that fourteen-year-old me who chose the seat next to the skinny girl who couldn't draw a straight line without a ruler.

"I'll never be like that with my girls, right?"

"Of course not, Ally."

The way I see it, you gotta hope you meet your people early, that the friend you have superficial things in common with as a teenager becomes someone who gets you later in life. Otherwise, you'll never find them. That person who understands where you came from, knows the shorthand, can make you laugh until you pee with just a facial expression. The free time you have when you're young, the sleepovers and dinners with someone else's parents, you'll never have that kind of time again. The only other person you get to know like that is the one you marry.

When I was twenty, I was asked out on a date by a friend of a friend I'd admired for months. I bought a new dress for the occasion, a yellow sundress covered in little blue flowers. He opened the car door and paid for dinner and held my hand during the movie. At the end of the night, he made me coffee in his studio apartment and then he ripped my dress while he pushed my face into his plaid couch. He dropped me back off at my parents' house and I slipped past their closed bedroom door and pushed that dress deep into the bathroom trash can. I never told anyone, certainly not my mother, and never went to the police. It would have been my word against his.

Sara was in New York at the time and when she came home for Christmas, I hadn't wanted to ruin the holiday. By summer, too much time had passed. And, by then, I'd figured out something else: As long as no one knew, I could pretend it hadn't happened.

Last year, I found his obituary online and breathed a huge sigh of relief. For two reasons. It had taken awhile for me to realize that by not pressing charges I'd left him free to hurt other women. I'd been beating myself up over that for years and it felt good to let it go. But the other thing? With him dead, there was no longer another living person who knew about that night. It felt even more like something that only existed in my head and if I refused to think about it, it didn't exist anywhere at all.

I've never told Karl. We met shortly after it happened and I had sex with him sooner than I usually would have. I wanted to erase that other man's hands on me, replace that memory with a choice I was making.

Karl was slow and gentle that first time. He kept saying "Okay?" and when I nodded, he'd whisper "Ohmygod!" like he couldn't believe how lucky he was that I let him take off my clothes and touch me. Even as our lovemaking became more adventurous, he still made me feel that way.

I sit next to Karl on the couch and point the remote at the screen. As silence fills the room, his head snaps to attention. He rubs his face.

Lucy's antennae headband is lying on the floor beside a box I'd begun packing earlier. When I started, the girls were sitting on the couch together, reading a book, little angels. I'd only had time to put three knick-knacks inside before Grace ripped a page and a scuffle ensued.

"What time is it?" Karl mumbles.

I reach for the headband and set it on my lap. "Almost one."

Trick-or-treating had been so much nicer this year, strolling house to house in a neighborhood. Last year, Lucy and I went to my friend Nancy's apartment complex, did all three floors. I thought being indoors would be easier, but it just depressed me. It was nothing like my own childhood. My dad had always been the one to take me, my mother insisting someone had to stay home to hand out candy. My brother was too old by then to bother so it was just my dad and me on those nights, a rare thing.

This year, Lucy had to wear her wings over her winter coat. Karl had the night off work and was able to go with us. I dressed Grace as a teddy bear and she slept in the stroller all night. Lucy and Karl walked a few steps ahead, holding hands. She'd ring the bell and look up at him, waiting for him to nod. "Trick or treat," she'd say and his lips would move soundlessly in support.

Karl reaches for the arm of the couch and starts to get up, but I put my hand on his knee and he stops, looks back.

"Gotta talk," I say.

"Is it bad?"

I nod and my face crumples. He pulls me in and squeezes tight. God, that feels good.

Tim: Thursday

I decide to place the call at 11:30, knowing I can use lunch as my excuse to hang up whenever we run out of things to say to each other. I rock back in the high-backed chair, imagining him puttering around the kitchen. Growing up, the only phone in the house hung from the wall next to the refrigerator. But maybe he has something cordless by now.

He picks up on the second ring. He's home in the middle of the day because he works the graveyard shift at the coal plant. I think he gets stuck with the worst hours because he's a loner. He says he doesn't mind.

"Pop! How are you?" Lola is curled up in a donut on my desk, in the space between the keyboard and the monitor.

"Not bad," he says. "How are you doing?"

"Can't complain." I get up and close the office door, suddenly self-conscious. Sara's cheerful pop music drifts down the hall. I sit back down and Lola opens one eye at me. "Happy birthday!"

"Oh, thank you," he says, as if it had slipped his mind.

"So, what's new?"

"Oh, you know, not much."

I clench my teeth. Didn't he know I'd be calling today? Couldn't he have thought of one or two things to hold up his end of the conversation?

"Snowing yet?" I cringe at the words coming out of my mouth. The weather, already? I fucking hate small talk. But, really, what else is there?

"No, not yet. How 'bout you? Still summer?"

"It's been cooling down a bit. This is when the snowbirds start returning from their summer homes. You can tell by the traffic."

"Maybe that's what I should be. A snowbird. Getting set to retire this year."

"Really? Is the plant closing?"

"Nah. I have a feeling it won't be long, though. The plant over in Stanton closed last year. Sorta feels like I'm jumping off a sinking ship."

It's hard to imagine my dad not working. That's what I remember most about him from my childhood: his empty seat at the dining room table. He was always gone. His absence was his most defining feature. He never missed a day of work, even when his wife was dying. I don't mean that as a dig. It's not the kind of thing I have any right to resent. The bills weren't going to pay themselves. "What will you do with all the free time?"

"Maybe I'll take a trip. Maybe something like you did."

"You gonna buy a motorcycle?"

"I still have that Gold Wing gathering dust in the garage. It probably needs some work, but I'll finally have time."

"You still have that thing?"

"Yep."

"I remember when you brought it home and gave me a ride around the block." My arms were so short they barely made it all the way around his waist. I'd held on tight, pressed the side of my face against his back, and forced myself to keep my eyes open in case any of the neighborhood kids were watching.

"I never did that again," he says.

"I remember that, too." It didn't matter how much I begged.

"Your mother was never a fan of motorcycles, and when she heard I'd taken you out, she was fit to be tied."

"Really?" I don't remember that part. I hadn't thought about that ride in years, pretty much forgot all about that Gold Wing. It really had gathered dust in our garage. It got pushed to the back corner and covered with a tarp, then other boxes. Every once in a while, my mother would pester him about selling it and he'd swear he was going to fix it up, but he never did.

My dad remembers to ask how Sara is. They've never met, so it never gets more specific than that. I ask about my Uncle Ted, his older brother, who lives in the next town over. My dad's just had dinner over there the night before and describes the casserole my aunt made. I like to think of him eating at a big table with people who think to invite him to dinner.

After work, the guys from the plant will take him to the IHOP for a birthday pancake. It'll be too early for a beer.

When the conversation begins to falter, I remember I have to go eat lunch.

Sara's made tuna salad. She's drawn a line down the middle with her spoon to ensure that we each get an equal portion.

"Did you poison mine?" I ask as I sit across from her at the kitchen table.

Sara spins the bowl so we've traded portions.

I place my fist under my chin and scowl. *"Are you the sort of man who would put the poison into his own goblet, or his enemy's?"*

She giggles. We both begin spooning tuna onto our bread.

I barely saw her yesterday. She'd gone out with Renee for lunch, and then I'd gone to Vintage Bike Night for dinner. When I got back, she was in bed, reading. I mentioned running into Delilah, but didn't say we'd eaten together or anything else that had happened. I'm not sure why.

"How's your dad?" she asks.

"He's good. Retiring this year."

"Wow. Is he excited?"

"I guess so. I'm not really sure what it will look like." Not that I really know what it looks like now. He works, sleeps, goes to IHOP with the guys. I'm glad there are guys. He's worked at that plant most of his adult life. I hope he's squirreled enough away to enjoy the rest of his time on the planet.

"You should invite him to come visit!" She looks up at me, wide eyed and hopeful. Her folks come out every year for Thanksgiving. Her mom visits again in the summer so they can do *girl stuff*. I can't imagine what I'd do with my dad for a whole week or even a weekend. Getting through a ten-minute phone call is enough of a struggle.

"Yeah, maybe," I say.

"How's your day going?"

I shrug. When Sara asks if I like my job, I tell her I enjoy the challenge. Sometimes, that's true. But, really, who actually likes their job? That old advice they give children about following your dreams, you can be anything you want, do what you love? It's bullshit. I mean, it might work for rich people's children, the kind of people who never really have to worry about paying the bills, people with a safety net. There's a difference between those of us who've been one paycheck away from homelessness and those who are one paycheck away from a loan from their parents.

I can see that there are jobs that would be rewarding: doctors, lawyers, teachers, chefs. But too many jobs have to get done regardless of whether you can squeeze some joy out of it. So, you get truck drivers and waiters and cashiers and cleaning services and telemarketers and landscapers. I've had some of these jobs; they're not all sunshine and rainbows.

David never really talks about what he does, specifically, but I think he pretty much builds bombs. He works for one of those big companies that's always competing for government contracts. I'm not sure I could do that and sleep at night, but then I don't have college tuition looming. (I don't even want to know how he voted in the last election.)

I guess we all work for the man one way or the other, even when he isn't literally breathing down your neck. Once, in an uncharacteristic moment of honesty, my old supervisor told me how you figure out how much work to give the underlings. Pile it on until they almost break, then dial it back 1%. Being my own boss is better and not just because I get to wear pajamas to the office, but I don't know anyone who loves their job.

Sara takes a bite of her sandwich and begins to tell me a story with her mouth full. She has to put the sandwich down so she can talk with her hands. Sara's one of those people you think is quiet until you get her one on one. Even when she's having conversations in her head, she has to use her hands.

I've finished my sandwich and she's still talking. When she notices this, she picks the sandwich up, sheepishly, and takes another bite. "I have a confession," she says.

"Oh?"

"I poisoned them both."

Of course, she did. I roll my eyes. It's an old joke.

Sara and I are making faces at each other in the mirror, brushing our teeth, when her phone rings.

"Ally!" she says, and I know I'll be asleep when she comes to bed.

I'm wrong though. About a half hour later, she climbs in beside me, looking serious.

"She okay?"

"Her dad is having surgery next week to remove a tumor."

"Like cancer?"

"They won't know 'til they remove it."

"Yikes."

Sara nods. "And also happening next week? Moving in with Karl's grandparents."

"Oh, yeah. That's big."

"So big. Now she has to get the whole apartment packed up in a week while caring for two kids under five and camping out at the hospital."

"Does Ally know she has a lot going on right now?"

"I don't think so. She was actually telling me how much easier things are at his grandparents' house 'cuz she doesn't have to carry groceries up three flights of stairs and she can make dinner while Lucy plays in the yard out the window."

"I guess easy is relative."

Lola hops up on the bed and Sara puts her Kindle away, giving up any pretense that she was planning to read. She drops anything when Lola wants a cuddle. She'll stir dinner on the stove while Lola curls up in her lap. She never just says no. "Ally's so close to her dad," she says, as Lola bumps foreheads. "He's always been her biggest fan. I think every kid needs that from at least one of their parents."

"Which one was yours?"

She scrunches her face to think about it. "My mom, I think. You?"

"Me, too. My mom."

She reaches out and touches my hip, flashes a look of, what? Pity? No. She loves me and she's sorry. That's all.

There's no reason to tell Sara about Delilah. It would just make future social gatherings awkward and it isn't like Delilah actually did anything. It might have all been in my head. And anyway, I had been clear. She wouldn't try anything again. If she was even trying anything to begin with.

I have never been very good at reading women's signals. I didn't kiss Sara until our third date and even then she'd nearly had to draw me a picture. Later, when things were pretty much settled between us, she joked about how I'd driven her crazy.

I never much understood the whole supposed thrill of the chase. I'd been mostly single since Carly split. I guess I was kinda gun shy.

I never really met anyone I wanted to give up being myself for. It wasn't until I met Sara that I realized it doesn't have to be that way.

I hated the part of the relationship when you felt constantly nervous, like it was just a matter of time before she figured out she didn't need you. I liked the part when you put all your cards on the table and she still wanted you to stay. I liked the parts other guys thought were boring, when you knew each other so well it got hard to pull off surprises.

When I turned forty, Sara threw me a surprise party.   That night, she asked me to get groceries, which she never did. She didn't drive and she'd never gotten used to the luxury of running to Walmart when she forgot an ingredient. She planned ahead. But suddenly, the night of my birthday, she asked me to go. The list she gave me was designed to make me go to every department. Limes, toothpaste, ice cream, wine. She didn't even drink. I played along.

When I came in and acted shocked, she knew I was pretending. It works both ways.

Delilah: Friday

I can't stop picturing Tim's face.

In my freshman year of college, I'd thrown myself at a guy in my Intro Psychology class – kissed him while he was in the middle of a sentence. I'd been so sure that he was feeling what I was feeling. How could he not? He pushed me away and I was stunned, horrified. I couldn't even hear most of what he said. The girl back home, his slow recovery from a broken heart – what did it matter? Humiliation pressed against my ear drums and his words seemed spoken underwater.

But that guy had kissed me back – just for a moment – and I knew that despite his stammered protestation, he wanted me.

This is worse. Tim doesn't want me.

I had built up in my head the deep connection we had. When he pulled away from me, I saw that. He saw it too. Technically, I hadn't done anything. With the benefit of time, we might pretend nothing had happened. But I remember the way he looked at me, as if I had wet myself in public. He was *embarrassed* for me.

I've hardly left my room since I got back Wednesday night. I've been replaying the scene over and over in my head for the past two days. My hand on his shoulder. His eyes frozen, terrified. Backing away slowly. When I think of the look on his face, my own face flushes with heat and my scalp tingles with shame. I squeeze my eyes shut, but I still see it.

It's making me feel physically ill. When Sadie knocked on my door last night, I told her I was coming down with something and part of me believes it. That's why I sleep all day and eat cold leftovers from the fridge while they're gone. I get dressed and go out before they return in the evening. Tonight, I come back with take-out and a bottle of wine. When I walk through the front door, David's on the couch eating a microwave dinner out of a plastic tray. I feel sorry for him, but sorrier for myself.

It hasn't been such a long time since I had a life with an apartment and a job and a boyfriend – all the trappings of successful adulthood. Or, at least functional adulthood. Now I have none of those things. I didn't pay rent on the first of the month so as far as I know, I've been evicted and my landlord's son has inherited my frying pan.

There's not one thing in my life that's going right.

David knocks three times, but he doesn't wait for an answer before he pushes the door open. I look up from my laptop as he stomps toward me and dumps a half a dozen catalogues into my lap.

"This is the effect you're having on my daughter," he says, and he stands there scowling at me with his hands on his hips. He looks so silly I feel like we're in a play – some melodramatic high school production – but someone forgot to give me the script. My lips twitch as I wait for him to break character, let me in on the joke. He doesn't.

I push my laptop aside and look through the contents of the pile. They're informational brochures for volunteer programs. Habitat For Humanity. Global Volunteer Network. The Peace Corps.

I look up at him. "Where did you get these?"

"Sadie's backpack."

"What were you doing going through her backpack?"

He rolls his eyes. "Don't tell me how to parent. You don't know the first thing about it."

That stings, but the assumption is familiar. I'm used to the attitude from parents whose children have ended up in my office. It's a defense mechanism. "I know that this is the last year you have to go through her shit and worry she can't make decisions for herself. So, you better hope you're wrong."

He crosses his arms and tips his head, looking at me as if he's amused. "You make it sound like growing up with parents who worry about you is such a bad thing."

"It can be when it's too much."

"I guess I wouldn't know about that. Sounds like you had it pretty rough, though. Dad went to all your soccer games? Mom in the PTA? Must have been pretty oppressive."

I'm struck again by the differences between our childhoods. Actually, my dad went to a lot of my soccer games. While I was in high school, he worked nights and was asleep when I left for school in the morning. He'd wake up in time to make it to one of my games and drive me home on his way to work. We'd talk in the car ride; he'd be jazzed and proud on days I'd scored, somber and encouraging if we'd lost. My mom worked in an office all day and never made it to a game, but she was in the PTA when I was younger. Thinking of my happy childhood makes me feel guilty now, and that realization makes me defiant. Whatever happened while David was growing up – it was before I was even born. It certainly isn't my fault.

I fold my arms across my chest and lean back against the pillows behind me. "Sadie talks to me and I listen. What do you want from me?"

"I don't want anything from you, Delilah. You're the one who showed up on my doorstep, remember? With a black eye and no explanation."

"You never seemed all that interested in an explanation," I mumble, avoiding eye contact.

"I didn't need one. I lived through it once already – with our parents!"

It's the first time I've gotten the slightest confirmation of my mother's deathbed confession and I'm forced to acknowledge it wasn't just the morphine talking. I look up at him and my chin quivers. I don't want to tell him how I really got a black eye and I don't want to hear any more about my parents' imperfections.

I look away. "Sadie's a smart girl," I say. "You should trust her more."

David takes a long breath. "I do trust Sadie."

"Then why aren't you talking to her about this?" I sweep an arm across myself, indicating the pile. "Why are you snooping through her things?"

David's quiet for a moment and I think he might actually be considering this. He runs his hand through his hair. "It's my job to protect her from people who don't have her best interests at heart."

My eyebrows lift. "People like me?" I roll my eyes hard enough to make my head ache. "I'd say you're misjudging the situation."

"Well, I don't really give a fuck what you'd say, Delilah."

My head snaps back as if I've been struck. I take a breath. "Alright, then," I say, slowly.

"I'm tired of your meddling."

"Is it really the end of the world if Sadie spends a year of her life volunteering?"

He reaches for one of the brochures and flips quickly to a page at the back, then holds it open in my face. "It says they require a two-year commitment for new volunteers. Two years, Delilah."

"It's not like she's planning to follow a rock band on a world tour. She wants to do something to make the world better. A lot of parents would be proud."

"I am proud of Sadie. I know she's going to make the world better. I have no doubt. She wants to be a doctor."

"Really? Does she want to be a doctor or do you want her to be a doctor?"

He's looming over me, shaking, his hands balled into fists at his sides. "You've been here for two weeks and you think you know my kid better than I do."

I shrug. It's probably the dismissiveness of this gesture that pushes him over the edge, but I haven't realized how close he is.

"This surprise visit has been lovely," he deadpans. "When are you leaving?"

I blink several times and swallow over the lump in my throat. I refuse to cry in front of him. "Tomorrow."

He nods, his jaw set. He bends quickly and scoops up the brochures. I imagine he plans to return them to Sadie's backpack before she notices they're gone.

When he pulls the door closed behind him, I squeeze my eyes shut and wrap my arms around my body, rocking. That did not go well.

It doesn't take long to get my things together. It's not like I ever really unpacked. My clothes are spilling out of a duffel bag on the floor in the corner. I stuff them back in and I'm ready to go.

Except I can't stop crying.

I don't know if David has gone to his room and I don't want to bump into him on my way out. I'm shaking and I can't catch my breath and I can't seem to talk myself through the panic. It feels like an endless series of waves crashing over my head. Tidal waves. I decide to make the bed, trying to really focus on getting it right so I can stop thinking about what's happening, what's about to happen.

I pull the top sheet tight and smooth it out with my arm. He's asked me to leave, basically. I mean, right? It's like Leslie said: I've *worn out my welcome*. I know I said I'd leave tomorrow, but I can't bear to stay one more second, knowing he doesn't want me here. I lift the comforter over the mattress and it floats to rest on top.

It's hard to imagine we'll even keep in touch after this. I wouldn't have the nerve to call him up. Maybe we'll be reduced to sending a card at Christmas, if that.

I kneel beside the bed and clasp my hands in front of me. My mother taught me to pray this way when I was a little girl. I haven't prayed in so long, I can't remember how it's done. All I can think is *please, please, please . . .*

Please, what?

David is the last bit of family I have left. For years, I've considered myself an orphan, but it felt better somehow – just knowing he was out there. My big brother. If everything went to shit, I could count on David. He was my escape hatch, my in case of emergency, my plan B. That's why I came here.

So now what?

Without David, I'm on my own in the world, without a tether. Adrift.

The wine bottle on the nightstand is half empty. I shove the cork in more tightly and slide it into the duffel bag along with my laptop. I rub the tears from my face and hoist the bag over my shoulder. It's quiet in the hallway, David's bedroom door is shut. I tiptoe to the hall bathroom, grab my toothbrush and sneak out the side door, through the garage, so I don't have to risk a trip past the living room.

It's cold outside, and dark. There are no streetlights in this neighborhood, just a dim bulb over every garage door, trying to cut down on light pollution so everyone can see the stars.

In my car, I stop trying to force myself to calm down. I watch the clock on the dashboard, give myself five minutes to freak out. And then I'll go. Where? I don't know. Away.

David's right about my meddling. I wasn't trying to help Sadie; I was letting her make me feel better about myself. I didn't care if her college plans were disrupted. I had no idea where I'd be a year from now. What did I care if she was in Africa or the University of Arizona? I didn't. It was just conversation to me, entertainment.

I didn't have her best interests at heart.

David does. Sadie's about all he cares about. I remember what it felt like to matter that much to someone. The memory has me doubled over, gripping the steering wheel as I wail. I'll never be that important to someone ever again.

I haven't said goodbye to Sadie. She'll come home in the morning and be disappointed. And then she'll forget all about me.

And David? He'll just be relieved I'm gone. It's his job to keep his little girl safe from bad influences. That's me. That's what I've become.

I look back at the clock; it's only been four minutes. It's nearly midnight now, and I wonder if anyone looking out their window might see me. They're probably all asleep by now, except the teenagers and mothers with new babies.

When I start the car, I haven't stopped crying.

David: Saturday

I can't sleep. Delilah has said she's leaving in the morning. Because of me. Because of what I said. I should get up right now and go smooth things over before she falls asleep. But I don't. I pull the pillow over my head and groan into it, try to lie on my back so I'm not tempted to look at the clock again.

It goes back and forth, the anger. I'm mad at her, then I'm mad at myself. I keep thinking: *what is she doing here?* It starts as a rage, but it turns in to something that resembles genuine concern: *what is she doing here?*

I shouldn't have been so hard on her. I know she's going through something and I still haven't asked her about it. What brought her here? What's wrong? She came here for a reason. I've actually specifically *not* asked her. I basically told her I don't want to know. What kind of lousy brother am I?

And what if Delilah's right? Have I made up this idea that Sadie wants to be a doctor? Am I putting too much pressure on her? I've allowed my ego to become more important than what's best for my kid, defending my parenting abilities to the point that I won't listen to anyone else. And this is what Delilah does, what she went to school for, counseling young people with problems worse than Sadie's ever known, thank God. Maybe she sees things I can't see. Things I don't want to see.

When we went to New Hampshire for Sadie's first Thanksgiving, it had been a battle with Janet who had never spent the holiday away from her own mother. She never had to again, either – the fight had not been worth it. Janet only spoke to me if my parents were in earshot, and then it was such a show of false sweetness, I felt like we were characters in a play.

Even my mother didn't seem as taken with Sadie as I'd imagined she would be. She spent most of that long weekend busy in the kitchen.

Delilah was a fan, though. She doted on Sadie, carrying her everywhere even though she had just begun to walk.

We did that thing at dinner where you go around the table saying what you're thankful for. I don't remember what everyone said. I imagine my father was thankful for the Patriots, my mother was thankful for God and I probably said the food. Who knows what Janet was thankful for that day, surely not her husband.

It was Delilah's answer I remember. She reached over to Sadie who was sitting in her high chair waiting for the bite-sized turkey and squash, gripping the little spoon she was just learning to use in her chubby fist. Delilah palmed the back of her head and they grinned at each other.

"I'm thankful for Sadie," she said and I regretted my own thoughtless answer.

I never should have said those things to Delilah. I may not know what brought her here, but I do know her heart is always in the right place. This is my sister, the social worker, who'd understood the true meaning of gratitude before the adults in her life had figured it out.

I roll over, glance at the clock. It's after midnight. If I want to have time to talk to Delilah in the morning before Sadie gets home, I have to get some sleep.

It's nearly nine o'clock when I shove the pillow from my face and feel the full force of the sunlight coming through my bedroom window. I throw back the sheets and stagger to the bathroom, feeling hungover. The bizarre dreams of a restless night linger at the edge of my memory, the only way I know I got any sleep at all. I take a quick shower and change into my weekend uniform of cargo shorts and a Henley.

I find Sadie in the kitchen.

"Are you just getting up?" she asks.

"I didn't sleep well."

"Where's Delilah?"

I shrug. "Not up yet?"

"Her car's gone."

Fine, I think. It's a relief, actually. I can make my amends later. First thing's first. I slide my coffee cup into the machine. My head is pounding from caffeine deprivation. On a weekday, I'd already be on my third cup.

Sadie pulls the refrigerator door open and stands there with her hand on her hip, seeming to wait for something suitable to materialize.

"Hand me the milk, will you?" I say and she does. She closes the door without retrieving anything for herself and sits at the kitchen table. She's already spread out her homework there.

I only need a splash of milk and then I'm lifting the cup to my lips. It's too hot, but I don't care, guzzling half of it as I make my way across the kitchen and sit beside my daughter.

Sadie looks up at me. I run a hand through my hair, still damp. "I want to talk to you."

She sighs laboriously and rolls her eyes. "Why do you have to say it like that? So ominous. If you want to talk, talk." When I don't respond immediately, she begins to flap her arms. "What?"

Sure, I'm the one being melodramatic. I reach for her hands, forcing her still. "I just want you to know that whatever you decide to do after graduation, it's okay. I'm on your side. I just want you to be happy."

She tips her head at me, looking at me with skepticism.

I sit back and sip my coffee, letting it sink in. Neither of us speak for several long moments. Her hair is down and loose, curlier than she usually wears it. There's a strand falling over one eye, a tight spiral as if it was wound on her index finger. I want her to break the silence, but I can't wait. "Do you still want to be a doctor?" I continue in a rush. "It's okay if you changed your mind. I just want to know."

Her brow furrows; she looks away. I'm holding my breath, telling myself not to overreact whatever her answer.

Finally, Sadie looks up at me. "I don't know, Dad. Honestly."

I bob my head with mock understanding.

"Right now," she says, slowly. "I really like the idea that I can sort of do anything maybe."

I let out my breath, grinning. I love her so much. Sometimes it hits me so hard, it's almost painful. I grab her shoulder and squeeze. "You can do anything, Kid. No maybe about it."

She rolls her eyes again and tucks her hair behind her ears.

"There are actually some schools with affiliate Peace Corps programs like NAU," she tells me. "So, I could still get college credit. I could do both."

"NAU?" I try to keep the desperation out of my voice. That campus is four and a half hours away. At least it's still in Arizona.

"Or I could always do a year abroad, like Delilah says."

"Delilah said that?"

"Yes, Dad." She says it like I'm a moron exhausting her patience. "I can apply to both schools. I have months before I have to decide. I might not even get in."

Now it's my turn to roll my eyes.

She turns back to her open textbook. "You don't have to worry about me so much. I'm not a baby."

"I know." I tip my head back, swallowing the last of my coffee. I stand and kiss the top of her head. Do children really believe that? That they can reach an age when their parents no longer worry about them? I bring my empty mug to the sink, thinking about making another cup.

But something is nagging at me.

I leave Sadie to her homework and make my way to the back of the house. I know before I push the door open. Part of me knew when Sadie said her car was gone. The bed is made; the room is empty.

Delilah is gone.

Her cell phone goes straight to voicemail; I leave four from the privacy of my bathroom. My impulse is to keep the news from Sadie for as long as possible, hoping Delilah will reconsider, return.

I walk slowly to the kitchen where I shift awkwardly in the doorway, clear my throat, and take a breath. "Um, so . . ."

Sadie looks up. "You want to talk some more?" she asks with a crooked smile. I hate having to ruin this brief moment of harmony between us.

"It looks like Delilah left."

She drops her pen and it rolls away from her and stops to teeter at the edge of the table. "What do you mean *left*?"

"Last night, she mentioned leaving today, but I didn't think she'd go so early."

"But, why?" Sadie's hand smacks the top of the table and the pen hits the floor. I walk over and pick it up. "Did you fight again?"

I hold out the pen, guiltily.

"About me?"

It's not her business what we talked about, I think, but it doesn't matter. She closes the big textbook with her notebook inside, stands up, and snatches the pen from my hand. She's left the room before I think of a response.

My cell phone rings and I answer without looking at the caller ID. "Hello," I shout.

"David?" The voice is small and familiar, but it's not my sister. "It's Maryanne."

"Oh. Uh, hi."

"I know you must think I blew you off. I mean, I guess I did, but I didn't mean to. I just – please let me explain."

I think the word for what I'm feeling is gob-smacked. I've never used the word before, but I think it fits. "Please. Go ahead," I say because I can't think of anything else, and I start walking toward my bedroom where I shut the door and turn the little lock in the doorknob as if that will keep Sadie from overhearing my half of whatever embarrassing conversation I'm about to have. Really, I had just started to shake off the rejection and I'm not sure I need the official kiss-off. Closure. In the moment before she speaks, I actually consider hanging up. It doesn't even occur to me to hope for good news.

"My son was in an accident." Her voice cracks and I sit on the edge of my bed. "He's okay," she says quickly. "It's been touch and go. We weren't sure at first, but the doctors are saying he'll make a full recovery."

"Oh, thank God."

"Yes," she says and she's quiet. "I had such a lovely time with you last week. Was it just last week? Time goes so strange in a hospital. It seems like it's moving so slow, and then suddenly days have passed."

"I know what you mean." I remember trading shifts with Delilah at my mother's bedside. There'd been an infection. She slept fitfully and I took each breath along with her, white-knuckling it until Delilah came to spell me. I was so relieved when the doctors finally let us take her home. I flew back to Tucson and by the time my plane had landed, she was already back in intensive care, then hospice. When I saw Delilah at the funeral, she looked like she hadn't slept in weeks. There'd been no one to spell her.

"I got your message," Maryanne says. "and I was going to call you. I kept meaning to, but—"

"Are you alright?"

"He was hit by a car while he was out riding his bike. Hit and run."

"I can't even imagine." I'm holding the phone to my ear with one hand; the other is at my throat. "Is he conscious?"

"He is now. It happened Sunday and he's just starting to talk. It's been such a long week. My stupid ex-husband was here, but only for a day. I mean, I sure don't want him here, but it's just unfathomable to me that he could be anywhere else."

"Where are you?"

"Albuquerque. I got a hotel room, but I'm never there. Used the shower a couple times, but I sleep here. If I sleep. It's terrifying to leave him even for twenty minutes. I've thought of you often but I never – I'm so sorry. You must have thought—"

"Don't worry about any of that," I say. "Can I help? Can I bring you food or anything you need from your house?"

"Oh, no. Thank you so much, but no. They're letting me bring him home to Tucson tomorrow. He's got a recovery ahead so he'll leave school for a bit. It's funny." She laughs then, but the tail end sounds more like crying.

"Funny?"

I can hear her blow her nose. I wait as she composes herself.

"Last week, if he'd called me up and said he was coming home, I would have been livid." I remember how she'd spoken about her worry that he wouldn't stick out his freshman year. "But now I'm just so relieved."

"Absolutely." I promise myself that I meant what I said to Sadie. I don't care if she's a doctor; I just want her to be happy.

"Can I see you when I get back?"

I lie back on the bed and close my eyes. "I'd love that."

Delilah: Saturday

I came to Tucson with a black eye and I'll be leaving with my arm in a sling.

It costs twelve dollars and forty-two cents to take a cab from the emergency room to the closest motel. When the driver tells me there's a place called the No-Tell Motel up just a bit further, I cringe.

"This looks fine." I glance up at the old-timey sign that still boasts the place is "air conditioned by refrigeration". I use the last of my cash to pay him and put the thirty-three-dollar room charge on my credit card, grateful for the EMT who grabbed my purse from the wreck. That's all I have – well, that, and the paper bag from the pharmacy. A prescription for the pain.

The blond woman behind the counter gives me a key attached to an orange, plastic square with the number eleven printed on it. It's a metal key that fits into a doorknob for the room at the end of the row across from an empty pool. I let myself in and drop my belongings on a little round table by the window. The furniture is old and mismatched, the bedspread looks like it's been here since the '50s, but at least it seems clean.

I pull the string on the bedside lamp and close the blinds. I just want to sleep, but first I fill a glass of water at the sink and sit down in front of the table. I pour out the contents of the bottle and line the pills up one by one. There probably aren't enough to do more than knock me out for the rest of the day. I swallow one and put the others back.

I reach for my phone before I remember it's gone. Having dropped one in the past, I can only imagine what happens when it flies around loose in a tumbling car. Rolled twice, or so they say. I don't actually remember.

There's a phone by the bed and I stand over it as it dawns on me that I don't know anyone's phone number. I walk back to the main office and use the guest computer to email Leslie. I'm drifting to sleep when the phone rings.

"Where are you?"

I look around the room. "A motel."

"Why are you in a motel?"

"A couple things." When I try to sit up, the pain in my shoulder is sharp and surprising. The pills only work if I don't move.

"Are you coming home?"

"I was, but I didn't get very far. Wrecked the car."

"Jesus. Are you hurt?"

"Nah. My shoulder a little. And my knuckles got cut up on the glass, I guess." I hold my hand out in front of me and flex my fingers. I'd only needed stitches on one.

"Was anyone else involved?"

"Just me." My clothes don't even have blood on them. I'm wearing the same jeans and turquoise tank top I'd had on when I left my brother's house.

"How did it happen?" Leslie's voice has a high-pitched nervousness in every question. I find it almost comical, but maybe that's the pills, too. Mostly I feel numb and floaty – like this is a drama happening to somebody else; I'm watching it on television and getting ready to switch channels.

"I'm not sure. I remember leaving David's and then I remember being in the ER."

"Where is David?"

"I can't call him. We fought. That's actually why I left."

In the emergency room, I had answered a seemingly endless stream of questions. Insurance and allergies and how I'd rate the pain on a scale of one to ten. When the nurse had asked if there was anyone to call, I'd said: "There's no one." That was the last of the questions and those three words seemed to hang in the air for a long time after. They're still there.

"Must have been some fight," Leslie says.

"Mm. I think he was right, though." I close my eyes.

"Yeah? About what?"

"Do you think I'm a selfish person?" Suddenly, the room feels cold. I reach with my good arm to pull the opposite edge of the bedspread and wrap it over me.

"A selfish person? No. I mean, all humans are selfish to some degree," she hedges.

"It's okay. You can be honest," I tell her.

I hear her take a long breath, let it out. "You have been somewhat more self-centered than usual. I've been hoping it's a phase."

It hurts, but I asked for the truth.

"Was that what David said that made you leave?"

"I think that was part of it. It got pretty heated and he basically asked me to go. It was all very upsetting."

"Were you so upset you got into a car accident?"

I rub my shoulder. "I don't remember the crash." I have an image in my mind of broken glass sparkling under flashing lights, but I'm not sure if it's a memory or a dream.

"Jesus, Dee. You're freaking me out. Come home."

"That was the idea."

"What are you gonna do now?"

"I think I'll sleep here tonight and fly back tomorrow."

"Is the car totaled?"

"Oh yeah. Shit. I gotta get my stuff before the impound lot closes at noon." I throw the blanket off and sit up. My purse on the table by the window seems so far away. "They're not open tomorrow. Everything I own is in that car."

"Are you sure you can't get David to help?"

I stand; the room sways. "I don't even have his phone number." I flip open my wallet. There, tucked behind my credit card, is Tim's card. I pull it out and sigh. "Let me call you back."

I watch for Tim's car at the table by the window. I can see enough of my reflection to know that my hair is a tangled mess. There's an elastic on my wrist, but I can't tie it back with one hand so I'm trying not to think about it.

When he pulls up, I rush outside before he can get out of the car. I don't want him helping me with the door.

"You're hurt."

"It's not so bad."

"You really don't want to call David?"

"I really don't."

He shakes his head, but doesn't press for details. I suspect he doesn't like to get involved in other people's dramas. He probably wishes he hadn't answered my phone call, but didn't know how to say no.

"This place is pretty retro," he says as he shifts into reverse.

I smile. "That's certainly one way to put it."

He pulls out of the lot and we trade stories about fender benders of the past, the childlike ignorance of drivers who've never seen snow, the fact that gun shots have begun to overtake traffic accidents as a leading cause of death in America.

At the impound, I follow a man with a clipboard through a field of broken cars. When he stops in front of a smashed-up hunk of silver metal, the only thing I recognize is the Bernie Sanders bumper sticker. *Hindsight is 2020.*

Behind me, Tim sets down the collection of cardboard boxes he's brought along. "Shit," he says, stepping around to the other side so he can take it all in.

Our guide marks something off on his clipboard and goes back to the office. I can only imagine the stories he's heard from the people he's met in this job. He's not at all interested in hearing mine. I scan the field of mangled automobiles. My car isn't close to the worst.

It's bad, though, and I'm in no mood to count my blessings. The Mini Cooper is unquestionably totaled. The roof is caved in and the windshield looks as if it's been battered by a hundred angry girlfriends.

"You flipped it?" Tim asks as he pries open the driver's side door. We have to crouch down to peer inside as the tiny car has been crushed even tinier.

I'm planning to answer him, but the view takes my breath away. Everything I had packed up in the back has exploded. The bag of clothes has split open and hemorrhaged t-shirts and tank tops and underwear. The cardboard box of nostalgia has come apart and no longer holds its secrets. The paper that reveals my SAT scores appears to be lying on the dashboard. And the shoebox full of photos I could never bear to look at has been upended, the images scattered like confetti.

I step back and turn away so Tim can't see my face.

"It's from the airbag," he says, thinking the metallic smell is what got to me. He moves to open the other door, mumbling something about a cross breeze.

When he comes back, he has a grin on his face and a photo in his hand. "Hey, is this David?"

Tim holds the photo out to me and I shake my head. "That's my dad," I say. It's funny: I'd never really noticed the resemblance before. David is tall and lean; our father was short and stocky. When he died, he had a full head of white hair and a beard. David and I have dark hair like our mother. But in this image, my father is a younger man, the graying of his light hair less obvious in the faded, blurry picture. The height of the photographer (me, as a child) makes him seem taller, the angle tilting upward and diagonal, cutting off the top of his head.

I'd gotten the camera for my eighth birthday. It was pink and rectangular and took film. You had to push your thumb against a button to advance to the next frame. I'd taken an entire roll of pictures that day and my father dove me to the pharmacy to drop it off for development. I'd had to wait days to get them back and was so excited when they arrived in the mail. In my imagination, they were going to be fantastic. My mom would put them in the photo album, next to the photos she'd taken Christmas morning.

I was disappointed to find almost all of them out of focus and unidentifiable. This one of my dad was one of the few I kept. He's beardless with a bushy moustache; it's his jawline that makes him look like David. My sweet, silly father is smiling, standing with a hand on his hip and the other disappearing outside the edge of the photo. *I'm a little teapot.*

I can see why Tim was so amused to think this was David. I'd be willing to bet that there are pictures like this of my brother – a man willing to risk looking foolish in order to make his daughter smile. I'd had a father like that and even though David hadn't had that father, he'd managed to *be* that father to Sadie.

Tim and I work at opposite ends of the car. With my arm in a sling, I can't climb around inside, so he manages. We stuff things in the boxes in a disorganized rush. I'll sort though it later. My laptop looks whole, but it won't turn on. The screen of my cell phone is blank and shattered. Much of my clothing is spattered with red wine. The jagged pieces of the glass bottle seem to be hiding in every corner. The checkered washcloth still holds my mother's rings but the larger band is gone and as we carry everything to Tim's car, I glance back but decide to let it go.

In the motel parking lot, Tim shifts into park and takes a deep breath.

I hate when men take deep breaths; it makes me feel like I'm about to get in trouble. I reach for the door handle.

"I can't let you stay here," he says.

"Excuse me?"

"I don't know what happened between you and David, but I'm pretty sure he'd kick my ass if he knew I left you here like this."

"Like what?" I try to shrug off his macho concern, but shrugging hurts.

"Like this!" He flaps his hand at me like I'm Exhibit A in the most easily provable theory of all time.

I release the door handle and sink back into the seat. "I won't be here long. I'm getting the first flight out."

"Fine. I'll drive you to the airport. But stay with me and Sara."

I don't answer.

"Delilah, you can't stay here. Sara and I have a guest room. If you really won't call David, at least let us take care of you. You're a mess. Sara and I will cook you dinner and keep an eye on you. You shouldn't be alone."

He says Sara's name a few more times just so we're clear, I assume, and I relent.

As he pulls the car onto the main road, I press my forehead against the passenger side window, cool from the air conditioning. "I really fucked things up."

"Ah well, it happens."

By 4:00, I am tucked away in a queen-sized bed with lavender sheets and a lavender duvet drifting off to the whirr of the evaporative cooler. It's like an air conditioner, but different. I half-listened to Tim over dinner. He held up the machinery portion of the conversation while Sara asked how I felt and if the food was alright and if she should check on me in the night in case of a concussion. Her concern for me felt oppressive and undeserved and confirmed for me that Tim must not have told her about my inappropriate flirting.

I begged off eventually, feeling like an asshole, saying I was tired. Which I was. I am.

Before I fall asleep, I remember to call Leslie back and she tells me about flights. There are several. We can talk again tomorrow when I'm thinking clearly and she'll book whichever one I choose.

She'll pick me up at the airport and I can stay with her until I figure out my next move.

Whatever that is.

Sara: Sunday

I wake to the sound of Lola nagging Tim in the kitchen. I hear the clatter of her plate on the floor and the *tingtingting* as she licks at her breakfast and the plate teeters against the tile.

I keep an ear out for voices. I usually sleep in an hour after he gets up, but this morning we have company.

He laughed me off last night when I asked if he thought we should be worried about Delilah hurting herself, but he's the one who got me thinking that way in the first place. All I knew was that she and David got in a fight and she'd gone and driven her car off the road. Flipped it, from the sounds of things.

I'm on the toilet when I hear the front door and by the time I get to the kitchen, it's empty. Tim's written "DONUTS!" on a paper napkin and left it on the kitchen table.

I hope he's going to the Dunkin' Donuts on Campbell. There are only two of them in Tucson, but they're the best. Back home, there's one on every corner. When I was growing up, we got a dozen donuts every Sunday after church. It was the only thing that made up for not getting to sleep in.

"Good morning." Delilah appears in the doorway on silent bare feet. She's wearing the same teal tank top as last night, her left arm in a sling, and I wonder if there's a connection.

"How are you feeling?"

She sits at the table and seems to think it over. She presses her right hand against the table top and spreads her fingers. She takes a deep breath, holds it, lets it out. "I'm kind of a mess."

I move to the edge of the table and set my brake. "Do you want to talk about it?"

She laughs, but it's not a laugh. There's something familiar about her mannerisms. She bites her lip and looks like she's trying not to cry.

"Sometimes it helps, you know, just saying things out loud," I say.

Delilah nods. "I don't know where I belong. I don't think I

belong anywhere."

I think of several useless platitudes. *Everyone belongs somewhere.* I press my lips together and hold them in. "Tim said you had an argument with David."

"Yeah."

"And you just left?"

She nods, looking at her hand. Her knuckles are scabbed, one held together with black thread.

"It's hard for me to imagine David getting angry enough that he wouldn't want to know where you are."

Delilah shrugs, noncommittal. "I can't call him. I've caused enough trouble over there."

"Is this about Sadie and her plans after graduation?" I remember Tim saying David was worried that Sadie might join the Peace Corps.

"That. And before that, too. I came here to get away from the mess I was making back home, but the mess just came with me. Or I made another mess."

"So, you're just going to leave?"

She sighs and leans back in the chair, looking up at me for the first time. "I'm planning to get a flight tomorrow. Tuesday at the latest."

"There's no rush. Are you okay to fly?"

"I'm fine. The shoulder's just a bit sore."

"Maybe you'll change your mind about David in a day or two?" I cringe as the words come out of my mouth. "I'm sorry. It's none of my business."

In my twenties, I used to give my friends advice. I remember getting frustrated the times they didn't listen. But, I was wrong about Karl. Ally was so smitten I'd kept my thoughts to myself so when it blew up in her face, I wouldn't have to tell her I'd told her so. When it didn't blow up, I was confused at first, then cautiously relieved. By the time she got married, I was just happy to have been wrong.

I no longer assume I know how other people should live their lives.

"It's okay," Delilah says. "It's sort of nice that you care."

"Of course. David's like part of the family. And you're his sister, so that makes you part of the family."

"Family." She sighs. "I've been thinking a lot about family

lately."

"Yeah?"

"David's all I've got left. And Sadie."

"But then there's the family you make as an adult." As an only child, I've always felt this strongly. Delilah seems unconvinced.

We're quiet for a beat. I look out the window where the bird of paradise is swaying like a rag doll in the breeze. We'll be turning the cooler off next week. And switching the heater on the week after.

"Where's Tim?"

I slide the napkin across the table.

"Ooooh. Is he going to Dunkins'?"

There was a time when I felt the way Delilah looks. Ethan had forced me to see a therapist. He'd actually tracked down the number of a doctor who took my insurance. All I had to do was make the appointment. And show up.

Everything in the waiting room was the color of oatmeal: the chairs, the carpeting, the walls. I waited exactly seventeen minutes for my name to be called. They weren't running late; I was early. I set aside the magazine I'd been pretending to read and stood up. The woman was short with cropped gray hair and a thick accent. It sounded German, but later she would tell me that it was Austrian. At the doorway, she shook my hand and I followed her down the hallway.

In front of her office, she turned to me. "Is it alright if Tammy observes? She's a student."

I took a meaningful pause, pretending to think it over. "Actually, maybe not," I said.

She blinked, seeming surprised I wasn't as accommodating as I looked. But she got over it quickly and ushered me into the room, motioning to a comfortable-looking chair facing a desk, and closing the door.

She sat across from me and started by introducing herself, describing her education, her credentials. She opened a folder and began asking me basic questions.

"Medications?"

None.

"Ever been in therapy before?"

Yes, in college.

"Suicidal?"

No.

She set the folder in her lap and looked at me. "Would you say you ever feel helpless, hopeless or worthless?"

I took a breath and gripped the arms of the comfortable chair. "Well." I bit my lip, determined not to cry. "Not worthless."

My voice cracked and she handed me the box of tissues. Beyond her, out the window, it started to snow.

Of course, the donuts are from Dunkins'; Tim knows me. He rolls his eyes at the mere suggestion he'd have gone anywhere else. We sit around the table with donuts and iced coffees, talking about our accents. Delilah is surprised I pronounce my R's.

"I went to college in New York so I haven't really lived there in fifteen years." I shrug. "I know I made an effort to lose it at first, but I don't think about it anymore."

Ally has a more noticeable accent, but even hers is mild compared to the stereotypes you hear on television. It's not just a stereotype, of course, but there's Boston and then there's the rest of the state.

"I hear it sometimes when she's tired." Tim places his hand on the back of my neck. I turn to him, surprised. I like that he knows things about me that I don't even know.

"What about you?" Delilah turns to Tim. "You don't sound like a character from Fargo."

Tim laughs. I don't remember him mentioning he was from North Dakota. Maybe David told her.

"I think it's one of those generational things," Tim says. "We've become less isolated in our communities when we're exposed to so many different kinds of media. It's stronger with my dad."

"How was his birthday?" Delilah asks.

"The guys took him out for pancakes."

"Well, you can't beat that."

Tim touches his back pocket as his phone vibrates. He takes long strides out of the room. "Hello?"

I smile across the table as the conversational dynamics shift and we become a twosome again.

"I use *wicked* twice a year," I say in a whisper, as if it's a confession.

"Oh, me too." That one crossed the New Hampshire border years ago, no accent required. It's a qualifier, used for emphasis. That's wicked cool. You're wicked smart.

Delilah leans back in the kitchen chair. "It's funny. I didn't want to like you."

I laugh, a startled bark. It's not what I expected her to say. More honest than polite. I think back to the dinner at David's. "I knew that." I say, remembering the way she had looked at me. "It's weird actually 'cause I usually get the opposite vibe from strangers. Like, often people are overly nice to me when they first meet me the way they might yell at a deaf person, overcompensate."

She laughs lightly and fusses with the strap on her sling.

"So why didn't you want to like me?"

Delilah shrugs and makes out like there's no specific answer. She seems uncomfortable, though, so I change the subject.

It's never just one thing. It's the bombardment of so many things that it gets hard to find just one thing left that isn't broken, lost, laughable or ruined.

At least, that's how it was for me.

Delilah takes a long nap in the afternoon and I take a book onto the patio. Unlike my usual reads, this is nonfiction, on the subject of happiness. Like, how do you define it? Have you figured out how to create a life that makes you happy? And, is that even important?

I've had people tell me to my face that if they had to live in a wheelchair, they'd kill themselves. Oddly, they seem to intend it as some kind of compliment, an acknowledgement of my bravery for continuing to get up every morning. It makes me feel sorry for them, if that's all it would take.

People act like having to use a wheelchair is horrible, but if we all used wheelchairs, no one would think anything of it. If you were an amazing runner, but everyone else could fly, you'd be pitied.

It's like that thing Juliet said at Ethan's wedding. Happiness based on comparison. I've had this thought before about walking. It only has value when you compare it to what others have.

To be honest, I think walking is overrated. I do everything I like doing; I just spend more time sitting down.

I hear the whoosh of the sliding glass doors and Tim's bare

footsteps behind me. "Tanning weather?" He puts his hands on my shoulders and the book drops to my lap.

"Mmm." This is one of my favorite times of year: when it's sunny, but cool enough to sit out in it. Tim doesn't tan; he thinks I'm silly. He sits in a lounge chair beside me; our bare pinky toes touch where the sun meets the shade. I think of the fish and the bird who fell in love. *But where would they live?* Right here. "How did Delilah know about your dad's birthday?"

"I must have mentioned it last week."

"When you ran into her at the brew pub?"

He pulls his foot away from me and leans forward. "We shared a table, ok?"

"Um. I didn't realize."

He turns to look at me over his shoulder; he's scowling. "Do I have to tell you everything?"

I raise an eyebrow and look him over. He's made vague reference to his jealous ex-girlfriend and I imagine that's where this defensiveness comes from.

"Of course not." It's not as if I tell him everything. Being in love doesn't entitle another person to every thought in your head. "It just seems like an odd thing to leave out."

He sighs and drags a hand over his face. "I know."

I smile at him and wait while he remembers I'm not that nightmare ex-girlfriend. He explains, embarrassed, that he thinks she might have, maybe, hit on him. He's not sure. He could be wrong. It was awkward.

Now I understand why Delilah didn't want to like me.

"I didn't do anything," he says.

I reach for his arm and squeeze. "I know." And I do.

In my twenty-third year of life, I decided I was done.

It was March. The previous night, my father had come to pick me up for dinner and I'd taken him down with me in the icy parking lot. Before dessert, I'd excused myself to the bathroom and emptied their medicine cabinet of old prescriptions. My dad took pride in how little pain medication he'd needed after his recent knee surgery. Mind over matter. I emptied several orange bottles, returning each to its spot on the shelf. I doubted anyone would notice they'd gotten lighter.

I got rid of anything in my apartment I didn't want my parents to come across, like the naked pictures on my digital camera of me with the guy who'd broken my heart.

I hadn't seen it coming. In December, he was talking about getting an apartment together. It was his idea. He'd returned from a job interview in Chicago with an epiphany: he couldn't imagine living without me. I was surprised at first, then started to believe that this was it. We'd only been together a few months, but sometimes that's how it worked. It was a whirlwind. I practiced the conversation I'd have with my parents, counting on support from my mother, the romantic.

Then they offered him the job in Chicago and he took it. He didn't even ask me to go with him. It turned out he could imagine living without me after all.

In fact, I was pretty sure most people could.

I had a calendar filled with nothing but wedding shit until Ally got hitched in October. And it was totally blank after that.

That night in March, I sent an email to Ethan, who was in England. I assumed he'd get it in the morning when I was cold. He could call the authorities, spare a loved one from finding me.

What I didn't know was that there'd been a party in London that night ending with a lover's quarrel. Too worked up to sleep, Ethan was online when my letter reached his mailbox with a familiar chime.

When my phone rang with his number, I was sitting on the couch with a rum and coke that was mostly rum, the pills spread out on the coffee table in front of me. My heart raced. It rang and rang and went silent as my voicemail picked up. I held my breath.

It rang again.

We talked all night. He yelled at me while I cried. How could I have thought of hurting my parents that way? And Ally. And him. He cried. He made me flush the pills down the toilet. As the sun came up, I drifted to sleep with his breath in my ear.

"Think of something you can change."

"Hm?" I pulled myself from sleep.

"Just one thing. Something wild."

"Wild?"

"Yeah. Shave your head. Marry someone who needs a Green Card. Move to Spain."

"I can't move to Spain."

"Why not?"

"I don't speak Spanish."

"So, you'd learn."

"My parents would flip out."

"More than they would if you killed yourself?"

That shut me up for a long moment. "I don't want to move to Spain."

"Where would you go if you could move anywhere."

"Somewhere without snow."

That's how it started. I spoke dreamily about the spaghetti westerns I'd watched as a kid, houses built from adobe, tanning in November.

Ethan googled it and told me Tucson had 350 days of sunshine.

"Do it. What's the worst that could happen? Nothing you can do would be as disappointing as killing yourself and you seemed willing to do that."

He was still angry; I could hear it in his voice. But I had to admit there was something freeing in the idea.

Before I go to bed, I check email and Facebook. Ally has posted a few dozen photos of the girls, mostly Lucy covered in leaves. I look at them all, click *like*. There's one of Ally and Lucy pressing their faces together, mugging for a selfie.

I can't tell you two apart, I type in the comments.

I have thirty-two friends on Facebook, only people I know in real life. I get requests from people I went to high school with, but I stayed in touch with all the people from high school who were important to me: all ... one . . . of them. I don't understand people who get nostalgic about those four years. I can hardly remember them.

Ally's father is going in for surgery tomorrow. I think Ally's unflappable; she's my hero. But the last time we spoke, she sounded . . . shaken. I send her a message: *Wish I could be there.*

I wait for a response, but none comes. It's after midnight in New Hampshire; she's probably asleep.

Ally: Monday

When the alarm goes off, Karl stuffs a pillow over his head. This is why the clock is on my side of the bed.

I sit up and take the covers with me.

"Five more minutes," he whines, muffled. He's such a child.

"You always do this." Last night, he promised to help me get the girls ready.

"Maybe if you ever let me sleep in on my day off, I wouldn't be so sleep deprived."

He works hard, it's true. But Sunday is family day, the only day we both have off. Yesterday, we took the girls to Apple Crest for hay rides and cider. The leaves had already changed from a few weeks ago when we got our Halloween pumpkins. There were crispy piles for Lucy to jump in. I took dozens of photos on my phone and uploaded them to Facebook before bed. In fifty years, will we remember the sleep or the time we spent doing things together? If it were up to him, we'd have nothing worth remembering in our golden years.

I lift my cell phone from the night stand and check for messages. Sara. I wish she was here too. She'd distract me, calm me. "Don't start with me today," I say to Karl.

He shoves the pillow from his head and touches my back. "I'm sorry."

"Mm-hm."

Lucy's in the bathroom with the door shut. I knock three times because we're trying to teach her about privacy, that it's something everyone's entitled to, even Mommy. But when she doesn't respond, I push the door open because that's rude.

"You answer when I knock," I tell her.

"Oh." She's sitting on the toilet with her underwear around her ankles, her favorite Star Wars t-shirt pulled over her knees.

I stand in front of the mirror and pull my hair into a ponytail. "Hurry it up. Daddy and I have to go, too."

"I'm doing number two," she whispers and I try not to let her see me roll my eyes.

I tell Karl as I pass him in the hallway. He groans and makes a bee line for the kitchen. I know he's going to piss in the sink. If only I had that option.

"You better move those dishes!" I call after him.

Grace is standing up in the crib, holding the rails. She grins when she sees me, her legs pumping with excitement. She can't wait to get the day started, the only morning person in the house. I lift her out and bury my face in her neck, kissing while she squeals. After a diaper change, I deposit her in her high chair in the kitchen.

"Daddy's gonna make you breakfast," I say, loudly, more for Karl's benefit than hers.

In the bathroom, Lucy is pulling a stream of paper off the roll.

"You don't need that much." I rewind the roll, leaving her four squares. She pouts at me and holds it in her lap, making no move to use it.

I pull the plastic hamper full of bath toys out of the tub and turn the water on overhead. "I don't want to see you in here when I'm done." I pry my clothes off and jump into the spray.

Call me superstitious, but I've found it's never the things you worry about that end up happening. It's always stuff you never thought of that catches you off guard. So I worry about everything. I worry the girls will choke or drown or be kidnapped. I worry I'll lose one and be unable to kill myself from the grief because I still have to raise the other. I worry that Karl will die in a car wreck or a heart attack and I'll be a single mother or I'll die and Karl will have to figure out how to do everything I do. Or we'll both die and Sara will take on motherhood out of her love for me.

Because I worry about these things, they won't happen.

Today, I worry about my father having cancer.

Half a roll of toilet paper later, Lucy's still on the toilet insisting her bum isn't clean enough. I don't want to give her a complex, not sure if this means she already has one, but I need her to get dressed. "That's what underwear is for, sweety. Just in case."

I bend over the sink and squeeze the excess water from my hair, wrap myself in a towel and go to choose an outfit for Lucy.

Everything is set. At 7:30AM, I'm waiting for the bus at the end of our street with Lucy. She's hopping around, humming to herself, excited to get back after a week away. I haven't yet told her she only has three more days until the move. I'm only bothering to send her today because I can't take her with me.

I have a class until 10:30. Grace will stay with the neighbor. Kindergarten is a half day, but Lucy will go home with her friend Caroline. I've written her a note. It's in her backpack, in the front zip pocket. I'll pick up Grace after my class and take her with me to the hospital where I'll relieve my brother and stay as long as I'm needed. Karl, who doesn't have a car, will get a lift from his buddy Gary, pick up Lucy from Caroline's house, and figure out dinner. This will likely mean McDonald's but I'm choosing not to think about it.

This is the plan, but it doesn't happen this way. While waiting for the bus, I get a text from my brother: "Come now."

My mouth goes dry. I try to call him, but it goes to voicemail. Now? As in, *now*, now? I look as far up the road as I can see. I can't leave a five-year-old alone at a bus stop even if the bus is due any minute, can I?

No, I can't. I announce the change of plans like it's an exciting adventure, grab Lucy by the wrist and pull her back toward the house, Grace in her carrier banging at my thigh.

"But I want to go to school!" she screeches, planting her feet and tugging in the opposite direction. I stagger between the weight and counterweight of my two daughters.

"Lucy, please!" I don't have time for this. It could be nothing. Maybe my brother is overwhelmed by hospital jargon or my mother's drama. He's easily overwhelmed. He's probably just forgotten that I have somewhere to be, that we *made a plan*, he said he'd handle the morning shift.

"Don't you want to see Uncle John?" I regain my balance and drag her along a few more steps. For such a little person, she sure does put up a fight.

"No, I don't!" she says and I can't really blame her. John has four boys and never seems to know how to relate to children without some kind of sport's equipment. His wife, Melanie, is a stay-at-home mom and she's a saint. Keeps him from having to learn much about parenting.

It's slow going. We're only halfway to the apartment and I can see Karl's beater parked on the street about forty feet away. If I put Grace's carrier down, I could lift Lucy easily, carry her to the car, and strap her in. But what kind of mother leaves a one-year-old on the side of the road? On the other hand, I can't very well let go of Lucy and at this rate, we'll never get down the street. I'm huffing and puffing, sweating, wondering if a neighbor will look out the window and take pity on me or just enjoy the show.

And still, the bus doesn't come.

I let go of the carrier and crouch over Lucy, gripping her tiny shoulders. "You stop this right now!" I yell right into her face. Her eyes get big, but she's still wiggling to get free, whining. "Poppa is sick!"

She stops pulling away from me then and frowns. "Sick how?"

"I don't know, yet. We have to go to the hospital. It's an emergency."

She stands up straighter and tosses her hair out of her face – a gesture that makes her seem suddenly so much older. Tentatively, I let go and she walks past me, her little black dress shoes clicking evenly on the sidewalk. I sigh, pick up Grace, and follow.

In the car, Lucy falls asleep in minutes. I make phone calls. I can't get through to John, but I reason that cell phones don't work in hospitals. I call the school to let them know Lucy won't be coming in, and Caroline's mother, and the neighbor who planned to watch Grace. I call Karl's work, but he's out on a delivery. Irma asks if she should have him call me or if I want to try back later. It's the *or* that stumps me and I just say "okay" and hang up before I realize I didn't answer the question.

Then Grace wakes up. Lucy sleeps right though the howling, God bless her, and I have to try to locate Grace's pacifier while she's faced away from me in the backseat and I'm supposed to be looking out the windshield because I'm driving. Eventually, I give up and let her cry herself out, which she does and by the time I park the car, both of them are zonked and I feel like I've drunk a dozen cups of coffee.

I unhook Lucy first. "Honey, I need you on your best behavior here. This is a hospital." She looks at me, sleepy and blank. She's never been to a hospital. I never even let her visit when Grace was born – too many germs. "Like church," I tell her and she nods, but I'm not sure the agreement is ironclad.

We take the elevator to the surgical floor and I nearly bump into my brother as I step out. He takes one look at me and starts sobbing.

The lobby is bright and seems to tilt as the elevator doors close behind me. I set Grace down carefully and press my hand to my forehead. I want my other hand free as well, but Lucy holds it even tighter.

"What happened?" I manage.

"He had a coronary on the table as soon as they opened him up." John covers his face, sobbing louder now. I've never seen my brother cry. I reach out and touch his shoulder.

"Where's Mom?"

He flaps an arm behind him and I bend to pick up Grace and make my way down a short hallway to the front desk

"Momma, what's a coronary?"

A young woman in scrubs sits behind a long counter. She looks up at me and seems to expect me to speak. I'm looking back at her, trying to figure out what I can say that won't scare Lucy.

"My dad had surgery this morning. Bob Dougherty. I'm looking for my mom, Judy."

The young woman's face falls for just a moment before recovering a bright smile. "Wait right here."

In under a minute, I'm facing a blond woman named Leslie something. She's wearing black slacks and a grey sweater with a scoop neck. I have one just like it in a slightly larger size, but mine is pilly. She must get hers dry cleaned.

She takes my free hand, the left one, and introduces herself as the hospital social worker. Her hand is so soft. She picks up Grace's carrier and leads me into a room with a pink couch and a coffee table with a box of Kleenex.

I'm having trouble thinking. It feels like there are many things I need to do simultaneously and it's vitally important to remember what they are. "You don't need to tell me what happened," I manage, jutting my head toward Lucy. "I spoke to my brother on the way in."

"I understand." Leslie says and I can tell by the kindness in her eyes and the way she presses her lips together that she does. She puts the carrier on the coffee table and motions for me to sit.

I pull Lucy onto my lap. "I need to find my mom."

"She wanted to be with your father. If you'd like to join her, I could stay here with the kids."

I picture my father's body in an empty operating room, under a sheet. They would have had to stitch him back together once he was dead, clean up the blood so his loved ones wouldn't be traumatized to look at him. I remember the last time I saw him, when he humored me by sitting down in the kitchen. Such a tough guy, my dad. "Oh, no, no. I don't want to intrude." Lucy squirms against me and I let her go. "I do need to make some phone calls."

"Of course." She kneels so she can talk to Lucy at her level. "There are some coloring books in that basket. Could I color with you while your mom makes her calls?"

"You wouldn't mind?"

"It's what I'm here for."

I stand up and prepare to extricate myself from the room. Lucy's already sorting through the basket of coloring books, no doubt trying to find one with horses or superheroes instead of Disney princesses. She waves at me over her shoulder. Grace is asleep. I promise I'll just be a few minutes.

Leslie exudes confidence and competence and calm. She could handle it if Grace woke and needed a diaper change and a meal. She could diffuse one of Lucy's tantrums. On another day, I might find her annoying with her perfect skin and non-pilled sweater, but today I'm just grateful.

I walk back to the elevators and give a cursory look around for my brother. Would he have left, assuming my arrival relieved him of duty? I wouldn't put it past him. I push the door to the stairwell and sit on the top step.

I pull out my phone with every intention of calling Karl, but I find myself dialing Sara's number instead.

"Ally?" The sleep is thick in her voice. It's two hours earlier in Tucson.

"He died, Sara," I say and then I start crying because it's the first time I've said it out loud.

"Oh my god," she says and then I think I hear Tim in the background.

"I'm at the hospital now."

"Where's Karl?"

"Work. I haven't called him yet. I haven't even seen my mom. She's with his . . . His body? I couldn't."

"You don't have to."

I cry some more while Sara listens. My sorrow bounces off the white tile and is returned to me. No one else comes into the stairwell.

"How do I tell Lucy her grandfather is dead? How do I explain death to a five-year-old?"

"I don't know." There's a long, comfortable silence as I listen to her breathe. "I'm sure you'll find the words."

"You think it's all a lie, right? Dead is dead. He's just gone. He's nowhere."

"I don't know what happens. Just tell her what you believe."

"What's that?"

"He's sitting on a cloud with Jesus?"

"Is that what you think I believe?"

"No?"

I'm not sure what I believe. I went to Sunday school as a kid, but my family was never really religious. We *believed*. We never talked about the details. "He'd hate that," I say. "He'd be so bored."

Sara laughs lightly. "I think children just want to be comforted and reassured that you're okay. She'll figure out what she believes eventually about all those bigger questions – you know, when she's six or seven." She pauses. "I think. I actually wouldn't presume to tell you. I have no idea."

That's Sara. She doesn't want to be the kind of person who gives advice as if she has everything figured out.

"He never went on vacation," I say. "Not even the beach. He was about to retire. I should have made him."

"Yeah? Were you good at making him do stuff?"

"Sometimes." There's some truth to that. He could be pretty stubborn, but I was the one who could talk him into the things he was unsure of. And Lucy. When we'd taken them out for sushi this summer, he'd been skeptical until he saw his granddaughter gobbling up raw salmon with chopsticks bound at one end with an elastic band. My mother stuck to California rolls.

Sara offers to come for the funeral, but I tell her it makes no sense. "You were just here. What would be better is if I could fly to Tucson. Maybe in a couple weeks. When things calm down."

"Sure, honey. When things calm down." She says it earnestly but as soon as it's out of her mouth, I realize how ludicrous it sounds.

"Right," I say, giggling. "So, once the kids are grown?"

"Right. Seventeen years?"

"Actually, it'll be longer. I'm pregnant again."

"Oh, shit," she says, but she's laughing. "Congratulations! When are you due?"

"May."

"Well, now I know when to schedule my summer trip."

"My dad will never meet this baby."

"I'm so sorry."

And that's really all there is to say.

Karl borrows a car and manages to get to us so he can take the girls home. We have to move the car seats over and it's only once we have Lucy buckled inside, doors closed, that we have a brief moment to be real with each other. When he holds me, I feel my guard dropping and I have to push him away to keep it together for the long day ahead. It's now my job to take care of my mother.

I smile brightly and wave to Lucy through the glass. We'll tell her together, tonight.

Tim: Monday

Sara's cell rings four times in the dark room before she stops incorporating it into her dream. She reaches for it as it goes silent, but it rings again.

"Ally?"

She sits up and I reach to stroke her back. I strain to make out the words Sara holds to her ear.

"Oh my god!" She covers her mouth with her hand. Her face crumples and she cries soundlessly, then takes a deep breath. "Where's Karl?" she asks and I'm surprised at her business-like tone.

I know we won't be going back to sleep. It's almost time for me to get up anyway. I reach for the light switch on my side of the bed and wince as the room brightens.

Sara turns to me and our eyes meet. Her brow is furrowed, her lips press together in a straight line. Her long lashes are slicked and clumping together from the tears. She closes her eyes and shakes her head and I know that Ally's father is dead. The details hardly matter.

"You don't have to," Sara says into the phone and even though I don't know what she's responding to, she says it with such loving ferocity that I know it's the truth. I reach for her hand and squeeze.

She puts her phone to speaker mode as she swings her legs out of the bed and transfers to her chair. I can hear Ally sobbing from New Hampshire, and when Sara closes the bathroom door behind her, I'm relieved by the silence.

My mother was sick for a long time. I was in the fifth grade when she had her first round of chemo. We were reverent about cancer the first time. We spoke its name in a whispered hush, if at all. We walked on egg shells when my mother's hair fell out and she insisted on buying an expensive, itchy wig that was meant to look like the hair she'd lost. The mousy brown bob. It fooled no one.

The second time, she let me shave her head with the clippers my dad had once used to give me the perpetual hairstyle of my boyhood: the buzz cut. By the time I started high school, I'd decided to grow it out. My father grumbled about it, but my mother would shush him. "I think it's nice," she'd say and she'd run her fingers through it absent-mindedly as I sat at the breakfast table.

Before I shaved her head completely, I showed her other options: the mohawk, male-patterned baldness. We laughed, we squirted shaving cream on each other, we refused to let ourselves be cowed. We'd been intimidated and careful with each other last time, and that hadn't worked. This time, even if it ended up being the last time, we'd be whatever we were, no apologies.

That afternoon I thought about telling her I'd lost my virginity, I'd fallen in love. I wondered what she'd say. On my previous birthday, my dad had given me a box of condoms. "Don't tell your mother," he said, and that was the extent of sex education in my household.

Would she be happy for me or sad that I was growing up? Would it remind her of all the milestones she might miss? Or would she be disappointed in me, angry? I imagined it, but I didn't tell her. I used a disposable razor to clean up the fine hairs at the back of her neck and she wrapped her head in a colorful, thick scarf to keep warm while her wig gathered dust in the closet.

I shuffle around the kitchen, the tile like ice on my bare feet. Apparently, it's sock season again.

As I'm making Lola's breakfast, I see Delilah in the yard. She's lying on a lounge chair under the purple afghan from the living room. Her face is turned away and I can't tell if she's dozing.

I slide open the patio door and she turns to look at me. She's no longer wearing the sling on her arm. "All better?"

"Mostly." She reaches for a mug of coffee with her right hand, the steam visible in the cool morning air. She nods at the blanket across her lap. "Is this okay?"

I sit in the chair a reasonable distance away. I'm not exactly sure what that is and I don't want to be rude. I decide four feet will do. "Sure."

"I was up early and I didn't want to make too much noise in the house."

"We're all up now."

"Even Sara?"

I nod and look away. There's a plastic bag hanging from the branches of the neighbor's tree. "Sara got a call from back east this morning. Her best friend's dad died."

"Oh, no," she says and she sets her mug down. "That's terrible."

I nod and we're left to quietly contemplate the death of parents, our own experiences shaping our understanding, looking like sympathy to the untrained observer.

After a respectful pause, Delilah picks up her coffee. "I have a flight tomorrow at 3:20."

It seems soon. Is it my job to talk her out of it? To persuade her to call David? I sigh. "We should leave for the airport by two," I say.

"It's the worst time to return to New England. Winter."

"Sara says it's the longest season of the year."

She pulls the afghan higher, hugging her knees, as if just talking about it makes her colder. "Yeah. Must be nice here."

"We get winter, too. I mean, sometimes we have to wear sweaters in February."

Delilah makes a face. "Such hardship."

"We try not to make too much of it. Too many transplants already. Soon, the Colorado River will dry up and there'll be no more free water and everyone will have to move back to wherever they came from."

"Aren't *you* a transplant?"

"I got more than twenty years. I'm practically a native." The neighborhood I live in now didn't exist when I moved here. It was considered the outskirts. Now there's a Walgreens and a Pizza Hut on every corner.

"And Sara?"

"A decade."

"When's the cut off?"

I scratch my chin and think it over. Before long, the only outskirts will be the public land, assuming the government doesn't sell it. "I think the gates closed after the last election. A year ago."

Delilah cringes. "Wow. Has it been a year?"

"This week," I say. The inevitable march toward extinction has been accelerated. Nothing left to do but hope to die before the worst of it. Enjoy what's left.

It takes longer and longer to get to the edge of the

developments these days, away from the traffic. I like to take the
bike over to Gates Pass, where the roads get windy and you can give
the engine a little gas just before the hilly parts, feeling the swoop in
your stomach, leaning into the curves. The tourists have ruined Santa
Fe, but there are still places in Tucson where you can stand with the
city at your back and appreciate the simple beauty of nature.

My phone buzzes and I slip it from my pocket, looking down at
the number, relieved. "Gotta take this," I say.

I stand and go back inside, closing the patio door before I
answer. I promised Delilah I wouldn't call him and I'm a man of my
word. But I wonder if I can get off on a technicality.

"Hey, man."

Delilah is sealed off on the other side of the glass, but I still take
the phone to my office and close the door before I say anything else.
David's talking fast. His weekend was nuts, I won't believe it. Good
and bad.

"Start with the good," I say and I sit at my desk.

He tells me about the woman he'd been seeing, the one who
stopped returning his calls after what he'd thought was the perfect
date. He'd agonized over it for a week, learning one of the many
painful dating lessons most of us learn in our twenties.
But, it turns out she wasn't giving him the kiss off after all. She had
an actual good excuse. This is the outcome everyone hopes for but
never gets when waiting for a call back. So as happy as I am for him,
I recognize the downside: he has not learned the lesson and will
likely hold out hope twice as long next time.

"I went to her house last night," he gushes. "I think she's it for
me."

"Whoah. Slow down, man. What's the bad news?"

"I fought with Delilah and I have no idea where she is."

"I might be able to help with that."

"How?"

"She's here."

"What?"

"She's spent the last two nights in my guest room. She was in a
car accident Friday night. She's fine, but she needed help."

"And she called you?"

"She doesn't know anyone else.'

"Uh, except me!"

"She said you were in a fight."

He groans. I tell him what I know about her injuries, the totaled car, her flight tomorrow.

"Tomorrow?"

"3:20."

"Why didn't you call me?'

"She made me promise I wouldn't."

He groans again. "She didn't even say goodbye to Sadie... Who is pissed at me, by the way."

A silence swells in the place where I'd normally express my solidarity with his frustration. "So, what are you going to do?"

"What *can* I do? She clearly doesn't want to see me."

"You're just going to let her fly home tomorrow?"

"She's a grown woman."

"I know, but don't you want to talk to her?"

"To be honest, I'm not sure. Maybe in a few weeks, with some distance between us, it would be better."

"Seriously? Wow." I don't have siblings, but I'm shocked by how callous he's being. For the first time, I feel disappointed in David, not that I have any right. It just seems cowardly, though. Isn't he worried about her? Isn't that what family's for? I tell him I have to get going, it's a work day. This is true, but the moment I hang up, I scan through my contacts and place another call.

I saw Romeo and Juliet at the community theater when I was in middle school. I went with my mother and I wore the gray suit I'd worn to my cousin Lisa's wedding six months before. I was allowed to wear my cowboy boots to camouflage the fact that the pants were a bit too short. My dad didn't come because he was working.

I was a kid who didn't mind when my mother kissed me in public or held my hand on the street or suggested I be her date to a play by Shakespeare. It was after the doctors had cleared her the first time, before the cancer came back. Her hair was short and spiky. Everything we did was a joy, a gift, a lark, a relief.

After the play, we went for cappuccinos and chocolate cake at a fancy Italian restaurant the next town over. I complained about the soap opera ending. She explained that it was meant as a cautionary tale about teaching the younger generation to hate before they even know each other, based on ancient family grudges.

"They're too young anyway," I said.

"Oh, I don't know." She smiled and looked past me out the window. "I met your father when I was thirteen and it felt very much like that."

I screwed up my face.

She threw her head back and laughed at the ceiling. "Just you wait!"

We worry about all the wrong things. The politicians and media have us on hyperalert for terrorism and mass shootings, but it's still the same old shit that does us in: cancer and heart attacks and car crashes.

"This is why people don't move away from the towns they grew up in," Sara says, endlessly mixing her cottage cheese, never lifting the spoon. She can't stop crying.

The three of us sit at the table in the kitchen, eating a breakfast that wouldn't have been possible fifty years ago. Now, everything's in season somewhere and you don't need to be royalty to have it flown in. Sara's having cottage cheese and berries from Mexico. The peanut butter on my toast was made in Brazil. Delilah's having a banana from Ecuador or Guatemala. And the coffee's from Ethiopia.

We complain about how things are without recognizing that we're likely at the apex. Food items from around the world, free and unlimited clean water, air conditioning in the desert. In twenty years, we'll be lucky if we can find sweetener for our gruel. Things will never be even this good again.

I rub Sara's back, gently, right between the shoulder blades. "I know." I don't remind her what she hates about New England: restaurants without accessible entrances, running into her elementary school nurse at the grocery store, snow.

"I was sure he'd be fine. I mean, he was in the hospital. That should be the safest place to have a heart attack."

There was a time when I thought of hospitals as safe places. When I was little, I'd had my tonsils out and my mother had promised nothing bad could happen there. But my mother died in a hospital and it lost its stature. The truth is, medical error is one of the leading causes of death. I don't say this out loud either.

"I can't believe I won't be there for the funeral. I can't hug her."

Her thoughts are cyclical. She keeps coming back to this.

"She has Karl," I remind her.

She nods. "I know. I love Karl." We all sit quietly, looking at the food we're not eating.

Frankly, we're even better at killing ourselves. I just read an article about the rise in opioid epidemic. Never mind the suicide rate. Here we are, the greatest country on earth. Why do so many of us want to die?

Sara drops her spoon suddenly, as if it has shocked her. "I should call Ethan."

Sara leaves and Delilah sits across the table chewing at a hangnail. I can't tell her that I spoke to David, that he knows she's here and isn't coming. But when I look at her, it's all I can think about.

"I should get to work," I say.

I didn't cry when my mother died. I'd known it was coming and I'd steeled myself against it, having somehow absorbed the idea that masculinity was about hiding emotions, or not having them in the first place. I was about to turn eighteen. I was a man now. I took it like a man and I was absurdly proud of myself.

My father cried. He cried in the hospital, clinging to my mother's lifeless hand, sobbing against her lifeless body. He cried in front of the doctors and nurses, in the car on the way home, on the phone with the extended family that had to be notified. I'd never seen my father cry before and didn't know what to say or do. Whenever possible, I left the room. At the time, I thought it was embarrassing, shameful.

When I think of it now, as a *grown* man who has learned the value of a good cry, I only wish I had been secure enough to cry with my father then, to sit with him at the breakfast table and realize that his broken heart looked a lot like mine.

Work is busy, which is good. A big project is due on Friday and I spend most of my day fixing glitches in the trial version. It seems to make my colleagues panic, but I think time moves more quickly this way. Before I know it, we're eating a quiet dinner: turkey meatloaf and broccoli. Sara and I stay up to watch stand-up on Netflix. Delilah turns in early.

"She sleeps a lot," Sara says. I worried things might be awkward between them after I told Sara what happened at the brew pub, but I haven't noticed anything.

"Maybe she's just trying to stay out of our way." I'm not sure how noise travels in this house so I find myself whispering.

"Does she have people to look out for her when she gets back home?"

I shrug. She's mentioned a friend picking her up at the airport. "I told David she's here."

Sara raises her eyebrows.

"He's not coming."

Her eyes bulge. She blinks and shakes her head. "That must have been some fight."

"I guess." I sigh.

Sara places her hand over mine and leans her head on my shoulder. "Did I tell you Ally's pregnant?"

"Again?" I cringe involuntarily. I make fun of climate change deniers, but you have to be in some other level of denial to be breeding these days.

"She sounded happy."

"We give them science-themed gifts for Christmas, right?"

"Yep."

"Oh, good," I say, like it's settled. Ally's kids will save the planet. Cool. We're quiet and I begin to wonder if Sara's dozing. I give her hand a squeeze. "There's something else."

She lifts her head and looks at me, waiting.

"I invited my dad for Thanksgiving."

Her eyebrows jump upward again, but this time she's grinning.

Delilah: Tuesday

There's a dying bird in the backyard.

No one else is awake yet and I don't know what to do. The bird is laying on his right side in the garden, between the aloe and the barrel cactus, his eyelids twitching. I go into the kitchen and fill a Tupperware container at the sink as quietly as I can. I set it in the soil beside him and curl up in a chair, faced away. His death is inevitable and I can't watch. I've done all I can.

My parents had funerals with closed caskets to spare their loved ones from the memory of their dead bodies. I remembered, though, because you can't spare the person who witnesses your death or is the first to find you. That's the biggest challenge with killing yourself. Even if you shoot yourself in the parking lot of a police station, some cop is going to have that image of you in their head forever. I think the least messy way to do it would be to fill a garage with exhaust and just go to sleep. But even that is bound to traumatize whoever discovers your corpse.

I pull my feet beneath me and wrap the purple afghan tighter around my shoulders. It's hard to believe that by this time tomorrow, I'll be waking up in New Hampshire, on the futon in Leslie's spare room with the sunflower bedspread.

I've been such a shitty friend for a while now and she keeps putting up with it, waiting me out. I guess that's the benefit of having history with someone. She's too invested to write me off quickly. I wonder how much time I get.

The sun forces the shadows back against the house. I let the afghan fall around me in the chair and stretch out my legs. The sliding door opens. "There you are. I found you," Sara says, beaming as if she's genuinely happy to see me.

"Here I am," I admit.

She rolls down the ramp.

"I love it back here," I say. "It's so peaceful."

She glances around the yard, nodding in agreement, then settles her gaze on me. "Are you ready to go home?"

I shrug. Last night, I packed my things in a small, black duffel bag Tim swore no one ever used. He pointed at my things in the corner and told me the airlines *frowned upon* garbage bag luggage.

"Ready or not," I say.

She reaches for a folded square of notebook paper in her lap and holds it out to me. It hangs from her fingertips it the space between us. "My phone number and email address. If you ever need someone to talk to."

I hesitate, avoiding eye contact.

"Or, you know, to share recipes," she adds, hurriedly. "I'm starting to run out of ideas for this meatless thing you started us all on."

I smile and take the note from her. I unfold it and read the numbers she's scrawled in purple ink. I don't feel entitled to them. It just doesn't seem right.

I look back up at her. "I'm not sure you'd be this nice to me if—" I falter.

"If?"

I take a deep breath and hold it, counting. I don't want to cry. "If you knew me."

Her forehead crinkles as she tips her head at me. "Do you really believe that?"

I nod slowly. I really do.

Sara sighs and looks above my head for a long moment, then back at my face. "I think I might know things you don't think I know."

I blink, startled. Does she mean what I think she means? I remember the heavy metal bat in my hand as I smashed windows, the lightweight notebook paper between my fingers now. Could we be so different?

"But I never even apologized," I say.

"Are you sorry?"

"Yes."

"Haven't we all done stupid shit we wish we hadn't done? Do we have to be defined by it? Does it mean we aren't likeable people?"

I close my hand around the note.

When I hear the slider roll open again, I expect to see Tim in the doorway. "David," Sara says. I don't know her well enough to be sure, but she seems surprised.

He's wearing khaki shorts and a green polo, like it's not a weekday. He steps down and Sara's head swivels from me to him and back again. "I think I'm going to go make some iced tea", she says and she wheels inside.

David drags a chair over and sits down across from me. "You okay?"

"Fine." I have an urge to wrap myself up again, but it's too warm. "Did Tim call you?"

"I called him yesterday. He let it slip."

"Yesterday."

He's looking at his hands folded in his lap, pressing them together like he's trying to crack his knuckles. "I thought you didn't want to see me. I wasn't going to come at all, but I changed my mind."

It's weird. I hadn't been expecting him at all, but that he knew I was here and didn't come, it hurts. "What changed it?"

"I didn't want you to leave without letting me apologize."

"You don't need to apologize."

"I do."

I cross my arms. "You were right about me."

David looks up. "No, I wasn't." His voice is raised now, shaking. "I wasn't fucking right, Delilah." He gets to his feet and starts pacing. "I don't know how you do this."

"Do what?"

"I came here to apologize to you, but you act like such a victim and I just want to shake you."

"A victim?"

"A victim! You've been so wounded these last two weeks and I keep telling myself that a good man would ask about it, right? But I can't. Because every time I look at you, I just see how lucky you are and how much you take it for granted."

"You think I'm *lucky*?"

"Yes! You have everything! You're young and healthy and smart and beautiful! You have no responsibilities."

"Oh my God!" I scream up at him, my hands gripping the arms of the patio chair. "No responsibilities is code for *nobody gives a shit about you.*"

"Oh, come on. It is not."

"It is!" I stand up and my chair falls over. "What do you know about my life? I have nothing! I lost my job. My boyfriend cheated on me. My parents are dead. My brother hates me."

He blows air through his lips and rolls his eyes. "I don't *hate* you!" And then his brow furrows. "You think I hate you?" He steps toward me and grabs my upper arms. "We had a fight, Delilah. I don't hate you."

He stares me in the eye and he looks so sad. It infuriates me that he thinks I'm a spoiled child taking my blessings for granted, but I don't want his pity either. I pull away and he moves to right my chair, sits back down in his. For a while it's just the sound of his loud breathing while I stand with my arms crossed, my back to him.

"When I was growing up," he says quietly, "I was afraid to go to school because it meant leaving her alone with him. I never went to friends' houses, never had them over to mine. I tried everything: being really good so he wouldn't get mad, being bad so he'd get mad at me instead, being quiet so he wouldn't notice us. My whole life. And then you came along and fixed everything. You were enough." I turn. He's bent over in his chair, leaning on his knees, talking to his shoes.

I think of him as a child. I've seen pictures. His hair was so blond then, it was nearly white. He always looked so serious in the photos. I thought it was charming, never thinking it could suggest anything sinister.

I sit back down across from him. "It wasn't me," I say and he looks up. "Mom got the doctor to tell him he was dying. So, he quit drinking."

I hear a flutter behind me and David looks over my shoulder. When I turn, the bird is standing on the fence.

Tim carries my bag to David's car and gives me an awkward hug at the curb, complete with back slapping. David and I stop for lunch at a restaurant with white table cloths and extra water glasses and a basket of warm bread to eat while we consider the menu. We talk more on this one day than we have in all the past two weeks.

We even talk about politics, which I'd assumed we were avoiding. I grew up the black sheep liberal of my conservative family. I always felt like George and Barbara were another set of grandparents we didn't see as often.

David agrees that the border wall is a stupid idea. "Besides," he says. "We need their labor. Americans don't want to pick fruit."

I groan. I hate this argument. It's what plantation owners used to say to justify slavery. "If staying in business requires exploiting people, maybe you deserve to go out of business."

He shrugs. "In a perfect world."

When he says this, he reminds me of my dad, the way he'd dismiss me as too idealistic whenever we got into a political discussion. It was generally at the dinner table and my mother would get nervous and threaten to leave if we raised our voices. We never did, though. These debates were intellectual, not personal. My dad was a good man; he just subscribed to a different economic theory. It was hardly a reason to ruin our relationship.

David and I move on.

He tells me Sadie showed him the essay she wrote for her college application. The topic is someone who inspires you. She wrote about me.

"Me? If she only knew how much of a mess I really am."

"How much of a mess are you?"

I tell him what I did to Lyndsy's car, expecting him to look at me with disgust and judgment. Instead, he laughs and shares a story about the week before Janet moved out, when he slept on the couch imagining ways to get even for her cheating. He considered scrubbing the toilet with her toothbrush, but didn't even end up doing that.

"Hell, I couldn't even make *her* sleep on the couch."

When the bill comes, he distracts from my lame offer to pay by handing me a letter from Sadie. I'm not sure I want to open it.

"You said she was mad, right?"

"Mostly at me, I think."

"Sorry."

David busies himself with the credit card slip as I tear the envelope open. Inside, folded in quarters is a page from the Peace Corps catalogue. It's the application. At the bottom, she's written in black Sharpie: *What's stopping you?*

I lean back in my chair and think about that. "You know, I don't even have a passport."

David signs his name and pockets the receipt. "That's an easy thing to fix."

We park under the blue departures sign. David turns to me. "You know you don't really have to go, right?"

I sigh. There's something so tempting about an open-ended escape from reality. "I need to get back and figure some stuff out."

He nods. "Maybe Sadie and I could come out for Thanksgiving." My eyes must get big, because he backtracks hurriedly. "Unless you already have plans."

Since my mother died, I don't usually do anything for Thanksgiving. Just another day. "It's not that. I don't exactly have a place of my own right now." Thanksgiving's in a couple weeks. It's hard to imagine I'll have turned my life into something less embarrassing by then.

"It was just a thought."

"I've never cooked a turkey in my entire life." It dawns on me that this might be an indication I'm not a legitimate grown up.

"Me neither," David says and I feel better. "We could go to a restaurant. No clean up."

"That could be fun."

"Think about it."

We say goodbye and I stand by the automatic doors, waiting for him to drive away. It takes me longer than it should to realize he's waiting for me. He won't leave until I'm safely inside the airport, on my way. I lift a hand to wave, hoist the duffel bag to my hip, and decide to go.

Epilogue: Saturday, November 11ᵗʰ 2017

They sit in the back row. The church is nearly full. When it's over, and the casket moves down the aisle with the family walking behind, Leslie gasps.

"This might be weird," she whispers in response to Delilah's look of confusion, clarifying nothing.

Outside, it's unseasonably warm for November in New England. Ally is easy to pick out of the cluster of mourners in the parking lot because she's holding a blue-eyed infant and wearing a black dress with an empire waist that highlights the specific curve of new pregnancy.

Delilah pushes through the crowd. "I'm so sorry for your loss."

Ally smiles sadly as she rocks side to side. Grace is nearly asleep on her chest. "Thank you," she says softly.

"My name is Delilah. I'm friends with Sara."

"Oh, yes. Delilah," Ally says, as if she's been expecting to meet her. She remembers Sara talking about her over the phone. She was the sister of Tim's friend, had stayed with them after a recent car accident.

Delilah nods. "I was in Tucson last week and I know how much she wanted to be here to hug you. I wondered if I could give you the hug she gave me when I left, sort of pass it along?"

For a moment, Delilah thinks Ally's going to laugh. She knows it's a ridiculous idea. Yesterday, she told Leslie, who had scrunched up her nose and said: "But who would it really be for?"

But Ally doesn't laugh. She hands the baby to Karl and opens her arms wide. She's bosomy and smells like vanilla and Pantene. She gives a solid hug and Delilah holds her just as tightly, not knowing if the hug is for Ally or for Sara or for herself, but it feels right.

"It's you," Ally says to Leslie over Delilah's shoulder as they separate.

"I didn't realize until I got here," Leslie explains, feeling embarrassed. This has never happened before and she doesn't know how to let go of her professional persona. "Delilah and I are old friends."

"Wow," Ally says. She remembers how Leslie, in her perfectly non-pilled sweater, made that horrible day somehow bearable. She wants to hug her as well, but doesn't. She's so emotional. Being pregnant doesn't help. She shakes her head. "Small world."

Ethan trots over with Lucy on his shoulders. She asks to ride home with him and Juliet.

Ally looks up. "Absolutely not. You need a car seat."

Ethan sets her gently on the ground and promises he'll see her there.

Ally turns back to Leslie and Delilah, taking each of their hands. "You have to come," she says. "Back to the house for coffee and snacks."

Delilah starts to shake her head, but Ally starts nodding. "Come on. We have deviled eggs."

Delilah laughs. "Well, who can say no to deviled eggs?" She looks at Leslie who shrugs.

Ally grins, satisfied. "Exactly."

In the car, Ally calls Sara to thank her for the hug.

Life gets busy, and they don't talk again until Thanksgiving Day. Sara makes the call after Tim's dad arrives from North Dakota with his Gold Wing on a flatbed trailer. The men are in the garage, looking it over, while Sara's mom bastes the turkey, covers it with foil, and returns it to the oven.

Ally is two hours ahead in her dinner preparations. She's making cranberry sauce with real cranberries, her father's favorite, even though he isn't here to eat it. Thanksgiving was his favorite holiday, focused as it was on the best part of every holiday: the food. He hadn't known the difference between corn flour and corn starch, but his appreciation for baked goods was what inspired Ally's love of cooking from such an early age she doesn't remember how it started.

She's stirring the sauce on the stovetop rapidly and can't talk so she hands the phone to Delilah.

Weeks ago, after the funeral, Delilah had mentioned her brother would be visiting for the holiday and they were planning to eat at a restaurant. Ally intervened.

This is the biggest crowd Delilah's ever celebrated with. Karl's grandparents are in the living room and Ally's nephews are running through the house. There are dozens of casserole dishes and pie plates covering the counters. Ally seems unfazed, in her element.

Delilah passes the phone to Sadie, who is supervising as Lucy sets the table. A water glass gets knocked over, and while nothing is broken, David takes over the call during the ensuing commotion. He's glad they've made a big deal out of Sadie's last Thanksgiving before she goes away to college. He imagines his life is about to get much quieter. He doesn't yet know that this will be his last year as a single man. He'll move into Maryanne's house after the wedding in September and when Sadie comes home from NAU, she'll get to know her new step-brothers over turkey and yams.

Sara pokes her head into the garage and hands the phone to Tim. By this time next year, the Gold Wing will be running like new and father and son will spend the week riding through Mexico. Tim will take his father to a shack on the beach that makes the best fish tacos he's ever had.

Ally gets back on the line and Tim returns the phone to Sara. At her recent OB appointment, Ally found out the baby's sex. She and Karl have decided not to tell people, but she whispers the list of baby names under consideration: Oliver, Elliot, Henry.

Sara closes her bedroom door. The kitty is curled in a ball on Tim's pillow. This will be the last Thanksgiving of Lola's life.

"I wish you were here," Ally says.

"Maybe next year." They say this to each other all the time. The last Thanksgiving they spent together was over a decade ago, before husbands and children and moves across the country. It was the first time Ally had tried to cook a turkey and she did the calculating wrong so it wasn't finished cooking until after midnight. They'd managed to tide themselves over with side dishes and the two of them ate hot poultry after everyone else had left or gone to bed.

Sara won't be able to visit in May like she's planning. Lola will be sick most of the summer and it won't feel safe to leave. Renee will come over weekly to give fluid injections, and when that stops making a difference, they'll decide it's time to let her go.

Sara will make the trip in November instead and she'll sit at Ally's Thanksgiving table.

Oliver will be six months old.

Delilah practiced her smile all morning, but when they call her name and she stands for the photographer, she's not prepared to be told to close her mouth. Later, Leslie explains they don't allow smiles with teeth in passport photos. In that moment, though, Delilah takes offense and her facial expression reflects a certain confusion.

At first, she's annoyed by this. This is the photo she'll be stuck with for the next decade. But the more she considers it, the more she thinks it's probably fitting. Delilah is getting comfortable with uncertainty. She's sleeping in Leslie's spare room, using her old computer to research graduate school programs, volunteer organizations and fertility clinics. There was a time when having so many questions about the future might have felt like a burden. But right now, she's starting to like the idea that she can sort of do anything.

About the author

Katie O'Rourke is a hybrid author who has both traditionally and independently published books. *Blood & Water* is her fourth novel. She grew up in New England and lives in Tucson, AZ where she writes, loves and is happy.

Check out her author site at **katieorourke.com** or follow her on twitter **@katieorourke78**. She's a contributor at **todaysauthor.com** and her own blog, **Telling Stories**.

Thanks

Thanks as always to the members of the Women's Fiction Critique Group, Gail Cleare in particular. I am lucky to have lovely, insightful writer friends who made time for me as I wrote my way through this, people like Jackie Bates, Ann Warner, Cindra Spencer and Mary Vensel White.

Thanks to Ani Difranco for giving me permission to quote her lyrics from the song, "Overlap". Those words are essentially the thesis of the novel.

A Long Thaw

A multi-generational story about the power of secrets and the unbreakable bonds of family.

A Long Thaw is about two female cousins who were close as children and reconnect as adults. Abby and Juliet were born into one big, close, Catholic family. But the divorce of Juliet's parents fragments this family and sends the girls in very different directions.

You might recognize Juliet from the wedding scene in this book. I write family sagas with overlapping characters. The stories in these books exist on their own and can be read in any order, independently from each other. I don't write sequels, but because all of my characters live in the same world, they're all connected.

Made in the USA
Middletown, DE
29 November 2019

79610783R00111